U0874663

‘Presently I heard a slight groan, and I knew it was a groan of mortal terror . . . the low stifled sound that arises from the bottom of the soul . . .’

EDGAR ALLAN POE

The Tell-Tale Heart

Contents

The Tell-Tale Heart

True! – nervous – very, very dreadfully nervous I had been and am; but why *will* you say that I am mad? The disease had sharpened my senses – not destroyed – not dulled them. Above all was the sense of hearing acute. I heard all things in the heaven and in the earth. I heard many things in hell. How, then, am I mad? Hearken! and observe how healthily – how calmly I can tell you the whole story.

It is impossible to say how first the idea entered my brain; but once conceived, it haunted me day and night. Object there was none. Passion there was none. I loved the old man. He had never wronged me. He had never given me insult. For his gold I had no desire. I think it was his eye! yes, it was this! He had the eye of a vulture – a pale blue eye, with a film over it. Whenever it fell upon me, my blood ran cold; and so by degrees – very gradually – I made up my mind to take the life of the old man, and thus rid myself of the eye forever.

Now this is the point. You fancy me mad. Madmen know nothing. But you should have seen *me*. You should have seen how wisely I proceeded – with what caution – with what foresight – with what dissimulation I went to work! I was never kinder to the old man than during the whole week before I killed him. And every night, about midnight, I turned the latch of his door and opened it – oh so gently! And then, when I had made an opening sufficient for my head, I put in a dark lantern, all closed, closed, so that no light shone out, and then I thrust in my head. Oh, you would have laughed to see how cunningly I thrust it in! I moved it slowly – very, very slowly, so that I might not disturb the old man's sleep. It took me an hour to place my whole head within the opening so far that I could see him as he lay upon his bed. Ha! – would a madman have been so wise as this? And then, when my head was well in the room, I undid the lantern cautiously – oh, so cautiously – cautiously (for the hinges creaked) – I undid it just so much that a single thin ray fell upon the vulture eye. And this I did for seven long nights – every night just at midnight – but I found the eye always closed; and so it was impossible to do the work; for it was not the old man who vexed me, but his Evil Eye. And every morning, when the day broke, I went boldly into the chamber, and spoke courageously to him, calling him by name in a hearty tone, and inquiring how he had passed the night. So you see he would have been a very profound old man, indeed, to suspect that every night, just at twelve, I looked in upon him while he slept.

Upon the eighth night I was more than usually cautious

in opening the door. A watch's minute hand moves more quickly than did mine. Never before that night, had I *felt* the extent of my own powers – of my sagacity. I could scarcely contain my feelings of triumph. To think that there I was, opening the door, little by little, and he not even to dream of my secret deeds or thoughts. I fairly chuckled at the idea; and perhaps he heard me; for he moved on the bed suddenly, as if startled. Now you may think that I drew back – but no. His room was as black as pitch with the thick darkness, (for the shutters were close fastened, through fear of robbers,) and so I knew that he could not see the opening of the door, and I kept pushing it on steadily, steadily.

I had my head in, and was about to open the lantern, when my thumb slipped upon the tin fastening, and the old man sprang up in bed, crying out – 'Who's there?'

I kept quite still and said nothing. For a whole hour I did not move a muscle, and in the meantime I did not hear him lie down. He was still sitting up in the bed listening; – just as I have done, night after night, hearkening to the death watches in the wall.

Presently I heard a slight groan, and I knew it was the groan of mortal terror. It was not a groan of pain or of grief – oh, no! – it was the low stifled sound that arises from the bottom of the soul when overcharged with awe. I knew the sound well. Many a night, just at midnight, when all the world slept, it has welled up from my own bosom, deepening, with its dreadful echo, the terrors that distracted me. I say I knew it well. I knew what the old man felt, and pitied him, although I chuckled at heart. I knew that he had been lying awake ever since the first slight noise, when he had turned in the bed. His fears had been ever since growing upon him. He had been trying to fancy them causeless, but could not. He had been saying to himself – 'It is nothing but the wind in the chimney – it is only a mouse crossing the floor,' or 'it is merely a cricket which has made a single chirp.' Yes, he had been trying to comfort himself with these suppositions: but he had found all in vain. *All in vain*; because Death, in approaching him had stalked with his black shadow before him, and enveloped the victim. And it was the mournful influence of the unperceived shadow that caused him to feel – although he neither saw nor heard – to *feel* the presence of my head within the room.

When I had waited a long time, very patiently, without hearing him lie down, I resolved to open a little – a very, very little crevice in the lantern. So I opened it – you cannot imagine how stealthily, stealthily – until, at length a simple dim ray, like the thread of the spider, shot from out the crevice and fell full upon the vulture eye.

It was open – wide, wide open – and I grew furious as I gazed upon it. I saw it with perfect distinctness – all a dull blue, with a hideous veil over it that chilled the very marrow in my bones; but I could see nothing else of the old man's face or person: for I had directed the ray as if by instinct, precisely upon the damned spot.

And have I not told you that what you mistake for madness is but over acuteness of the senses? – now, I say, there came to my ears a low, dull, quick sound, such as a watch makes when enveloped in cotton. I knew *that* sound well, too. It was the beating of the old man's heart. It increased my fury, as the beating of a drum stimulates the soldier into courage.

But even yet I refrained and kept still. I scarcely breathed. I held the lantern motionless. I tried how steadily I could maintain the ray upon the eye. Meantime the hellish tattoo of the heart increased. It grew quicker and quicker, and louder and louder every instant. The old man's terror *must* have been extreme! It grew louder, I say, louder every moment! – do you mark me well? I have told you that I am nervous: so I am. And now at the dead hour of the night, amid the dreadful silence of that old house, so strange a noise as this excited me to uncontrollable terror. Yet, for some minutes longer I refrained and stood still. But the beating grew louder, louder! I thought the heart must burst. And now a new anxiety seized me – the sound would be heard by a neighbour! The old man's hour had come! With a loud yell, I threw open the lantern and leaped into the room. He shrieked once – once only. In an instant I dragged him to the floor, and pulled the heavy bed over him. I then smiled gaily, to find the deed so far done. But, for many minutes, the heart beat on with a muffled sound. This, however, did not vex me; it would not be heard through the wall. At length it ceased. The old man was dead. I removed the bed and examined the corpse. Yes, he was stone, stone dead. I placed my hand upon the heart and held it there many minutes. There was no pulsation. He was stone dead. His eye would trouble me no more.

If still you think me mad, you will think so no longer when I describe the wise precautions I took for the concealment of the body. The night waned; and I worked hastily, but in silence. First of all I dismembered the corpse. I cut off the head and the arms and the legs.

I then took up three planks from the flooring of the chamber, and deposited all between the scantlings. I then replaced the boards so cleverly, so cunningly, that no human eye – not even *his* – could have detected any thing wrong. There was nothing to wash out – no stain of any kind – no blood-spot whatever. I had been too wary for that. A tub had caught all – ha! ha!

When I had made an end of these labours, it was four o'clock – still dark as midnight. As the bell sounded the hour, there came a knocking at the street door. I went down to open it with a light heart, – for what had I *now* to fear? There entered three men, who introduced themselves, with perfect suavity, as officers of the police. A shriek had been heard by a neighbour during the night; suspicion of foul play had been aroused; information had been lodged at the police office, and they (the officers) had been deputed to search the premises.

I smiled, – for *what* had I to fear? I bade the gentlemen

welcome. The shriek, I said, was my own in a dream. The old man, I mentioned, was absent in the country. I took my visitors all over the house. I bade them search – search *well*. I led them, at length, to *his* chamber. I showed them his treasures, secure, undisturbed. In the enthusiasm of my confidence, I brought chairs into the room, and desired them *here* to rest from their fatigues, while I myself, in the wild audacity of my perfect triumph, placed my own seat upon the very spot beneath which reposed the corpse of the victim.

The officers were satisfied. My *manner* had convinced them. I was singularly at ease. They sat, and while I answered cheerily, they chatted of familiar things. But, ere long, I felt myself getting pale and wished them gone. My head ached, and I fancied a ringing in my ears: but still they sat and still chatted. The ringing became more distinct: – it continued and became more distinct: I talked more freely to get rid of the feeling: but it continued and gained definiteness – until, at length, I found that the noise was *not* within my ears.

No doubt I now grew *very* pale; – but I talked more fluently, and with a heightened voice. Yet the sound increased – and what could I do? It was *a low, dull, quick sound – much such a sound as a watch makes when enveloped in cotton*. I gasped for breath – and yet the officers heard it not. I talked more quickly – more vehemently; but the noise steadily increased. I arose and argued about trifles, in a high key and with violent gesticulations; but the noise steadily increased. Why *would* they not be gone? I paced the floor to and fro with heavy strides, as if excited to fury by the observations of the men – but the noise steadily increased. Oh God! what *could* I do? I foamed – I raved – I swore! I swung the chair upon which I had been sitting, and grated it upon the boards, but the noise arose over all and continually increased. It grew louder – louder – *louder*! And still the men chatted pleasantly, and smiled. Was it possible they heard not? Almighty God! – no, no! They heard! – they suspected! – they *knew*! – they were making a mockery of my horror! – this I thought, and this I think. But anything was better than this agony! Anything was more tolerable than this derision! I could bear those hypocritical smiles no longer! I felt that I must scream or die! and now – again! – hark! louder! louder! louder! *louder*!

'Villains!' I shrieked, 'dissemble no more! I admit the deed! – tear up the planks! here, here! – it is the beating of his hideous heart!'

The Fall of the House of Usher

Son coeur est un luth suspendu;
Sitôt qu'on le touche il résonne.
DE BÉRANGER

During the whole of a dull, dark, and soundless day in the autumn of the year, when the clouds hung oppressively low in the heavens, I had been passing alone, on horseback, through a singularly dreary tract of country; and at length found myself, as the shades of the evening drew on, within view of the melancholy House of Usher. I know not how it was – but, with the first glimpse of the building, a sense of insufferable gloom pervaded my spirit. I say insufferable; for the feeling was unrelieved by any of that half-pleasurable, because poetic, sentiment, with which the mind usually receives even the sternest natural images of the desolate or terrible. I looked upon the scene before me – upon the mere house, and the simple landscape features of the domain – upon the bleak walls – upon the vacant eye-like windows – upon a few rank sedges – and upon a few white trunks of decayed trees – with an utter depression of soul which I can compare to no earthly sensation more properly than to the afterdream of the reveller upon opium – the bitter lapse into everyday life – the hideous dropping off of the veil. There was an iciness, a sinking, a sickening of the heart – an unredeemed dreariness of thought which no goading of the imagination could torture into aught of the sublime. What was it – I paused to think – what was it that so unnerved me in the contemplation of the House of Usher? It was a mystery all insoluble; nor could I grapple with the shadowy fancies that crowded upon me as I pondered. I was forced to fall back upon the unsatisfactory conclusion, that while, beyond doubt, there *are* combinations of very simple natural objects which have the power of thus affecting us, still the analysis of this power lies among considerations beyond our depth. It was possible, I reflected, that a mere different arrangement of the particulars of the scene, of the details of the picture, would be sufficient to modify, or perhaps to annihilate its capacity for sorrowful impression; and, acting upon this idea, I reined my horse to the precipitous brink of a black and lurid tarn that lay in unruffled lustre by the dwelling, and gazed down – but with a shudder even more thrilling than before – upon the remodelled and inverted images of the gray sedge, and the ghastly tree-stems, and the vacant and eye-like windows.

Nevertheless, in this mansion of gloom I now proposed to myself a sojourn of some weeks. Its proprietor,

Roderick Usher, had been one of my boon companions in boyhood; but many years had elapsed since our last meeting. A letter, however, had lately reached me in a distant part of the country – a letter from him – which, in its wildly importunate nature, had admitted of no other than a personal reply. The MS. gave evidence of nervous agitation. The writer spoke of acute bodily illness – of a mental disorder which oppressed him – and of an earnest desire to see me, as his best, and indeed his only personal friend, with a view of attempting, by the cheerfulness of my society, some alleviation of his malady. It was the manner in which all this, and much more, was said – it was the apparent *heart* that went with his request – which allowed me no room for hesitation; and I accordingly obeyed forthwith what I still considered a very singular summons.

Although, as boys, we had been even intimate associates, yet I really knew little of my friend. His reserve had been always excessive and habitual. I was aware, however, that his very ancient family had been noted, time out of mind, for a peculiar sensibility of temperament, displaying itself, through long ages, in many works of exalted art, and manifested, of late, in repeated deeds of munificent yet unobtrusive charity, as well as in a passionate devotion to the intricacies, perhaps even more than to the orthodox and easily recognisable beauties, of musical science. I had learned, too, the very remarkable fact, that the stem of the Usher race, all time-honoured as it was, had put forth, at no period, any enduring branch; in other words, that the entire family lay in the direct line of descent, and had always, with very trifling and very temporary variation, so lain. It was this deficiency, I considered, while running over in thought the perfect keeping of the character of the premises with the accredited character of the people, and while speculating upon the possible influence which the one, in the long lapse of centuries, might have exercised upon the other – it was this deficiency, perhaps, of collateral issue, and the consequent undeviating transmission, from sire to son, of the patrimony with the name, which had, at length, so identified the two as to merge the original title of the estate in the quaint and equivocal appellation of the 'House of Usher' – an appellation which seemed to include, in the minds of the peasantry who used it, both the family and the family mansion.

I have said that the sole effect of my somewhat childish experiment – that of looking down within the tarn – had been to deepen the first singular impression. There can be no doubt that the consciousness of the rapid increase of my superstition – for why should I not so term it? – served mainly to accelerate the increase itself. Such, I have long known, is the paradoxical law of all sentiments having terror as a basis. And it might have been for this reason only, that, when I again uplifted my eyes to the house itself, from its image in the pool, there grew in my mind a strange fancy – a fancy so ridiculous, indeed, that I but mention it to show the vivid force of the sensations which oppressed me. I had so worked upon my imagination as really to believe that about the whole mansion and domain there hung an atmosphere peculiar to themselves and their immediate vicinity – an atmosphere which had no affinity with the air of heaven, but which had reeked up from the decayed trees, and the gray wall, and the silent tarn – a pestilent and mystic vapour, dull, sluggish, faintly discernible, and leaden-hued.

Shaking off from my spirit what *must* have been a dream, I scanned more narrowly the real aspect of the building. Its principal feature seemed to be that of an excessive antiquity. The discoloration of ages had been great. Minute fungi overspread the whole exterior, hanging in a fine tangled web-work from the eaves. Yet all this was apart from any extraordinary dilapidation. No portion of the masonry had fallen; and there appeared to be a wild inconsistency between its still perfect adaptation of parts, and the crumbling condition of the individual stones. In this there was much that reminded me of the specious totality of old wood-work which has rotted for long years in some neglected vault, with no disturbance from the breath of the external air. Beyond this indication of extensive decay, however, the fabric gave little token of instability. Perhaps the eye of a scrutinising observer might have discovered a barely perceptible fissure, which, extending from the roof of the building in front, made its way down the wall in a zigzag direction, until it became lost in the sullen waters of the tarn.

Noticing these things, I rode over a short causeway to the house. A servant in waiting took my horse and I entered the Gothic archway of the hall. A valet, of stealthy step, thence conducted me, in silence, through many dark and intricate passages in my progress to the *studio* of his master. Much that I encountered on the way contributed, I know not how, to heighten the vague sentiments of which I have already spoken. While the objects around me – while the carvings of the ceilings, the sombre tapestries of the walls, the ebon blackness of the floors, and the phantasmagoric armorial trophies which rattled as I strode, were but matters to which, or to such as which, I had been accustomed from my infancy – while I hesitated not to acknowledge how familiar was all this – I still wondered to find how unfamiliar were the fancies which ordinary images were stirring up. On one of the staircases, I met the physician of the family. His countenance, I thought, wore a mingled expression of low cunning and perplexity. He accosted me with trepidation and passed on. The valet now threw open a door and ushered me into the presence of his master.

The room in which I found myself was very large and lofty. The windows were long, narrow, and pointed, and at so vast a distance from the black oaken floor as to be altogether inaccessible from within. Feeble gleams of encrimsoned light made their way through the trellised panes, and served to render sufficiently distinct the more prominent objects around; the eye, however, struggled in vain to reach the remoter angles of the chamber, or the recesses of the vaulted and fretted ceiling. Dark draperies hung upon the walls. The general furniture was profuse, comfortless, antique, and tattered. Many books and musical instruments lay scattered about, but failed to give any vitality to the scene. I felt that I breathed an atmosphere of sorrow. An air of stern, deep, and irredeemable gloom hung over and pervaded all.

Upon my entrance, Usher arose from a sofa on which he had been lying at full length, and greeted me with a vivacious warmth which had much in it, I at first thought, of an overdone cordiality – of the constrained effort of the *ennuyé* man of the world. A glance, however, at his countenance, convinced me of his perfect sincerity. We sat down; and for some moments, while he spoke not, I gazed upon him with a feeling half of pity, half of awe. Surely, man had never before so terribly altered, in so brief a period, as had Roderick Usher! It was with difficulty that I could bring myself to admit the identity of the wan being before me with the companion of my early boyhood. Yet the character of his face had been at all times remarkable. A cadaverousness of complexion; an eye large, liquid, and luminous beyond comparison; lips somewhat thin and very pallid, but of a surpassingly beautiful curve; a nose of a delicate Hebrew model, but with a breadth of nostril unusual in similar formations; a finely moulded chin, speaking, in its want of prominence, of a want of moral energy; hair of a more than web-like softness and tenuity; these features, with an inordinate expansion above the regions of the temple, made up altogether a countenance not easily to be forgotten. And now in the mere exaggeration of the prevailing character of these features, and of the expression they were wont to convey, lay so much of change that I doubted to whom I spoke. The now ghastly pallor of the skin, and the now miraculous lustre of the eye, above all things startled and even awed me. The silken hair, too, had been suffered to grow all unheeded, and as, in its wild gossamer texture, it floated rather than fell about the face, I could not, even with effort, connect its Arabesque expression with any idea of simple humanity.

In the manner of my friend I was at once struck with an incoherence – an inconsistency; and I soon found this to arise from a series of feeble and futile struggles to overcome an habitual trepidancy – an excessive nervous agitation. For something of this nature I had indeed been prepared, no less by his letter, than by reminiscences of certain boyish traits, and by conclusions deduced from his peculiar physical conformation and temperament. His action was alternately vivacious and sullen. His voice varied rapidly from a tremulous indecision (when the animal spirits seemed utterly in abeyance) to that species of energetic concision – that abrupt, weighty, unhurried, and hollow-sounding enunciation – that leaden, self-balanced and perfectly modulated guttural utterance, which may be observed in the lost drunkard, or the irreclaimable eater of opium, during the periods of his most intense excitement.

It was thus that he spoke of the object of my visit, of his earnest desire to see me, and of the solace he expected me to afford him. He entered, at some length, into what he conceived to be the nature of his malady. It was, he said, a constitutional and a family evil, and one for which he despaired to find a remedy – a mere nervous affection, he immediately added, which would undoubtedly soon pass off. It displayed itself in a host of unnatural sensations. Some of these, as he detailed them, interested and bewildered me; although, perhaps, the terms, and the general manner of the narration had their weight. He suffered much from a morbid acuteness of the senses; the most insipid food was alone endurable; he could wear only garments of certain texture; the odours of all flowers were oppressive; his eyes were tortured by even a faint light; and there were but peculiar sounds, and these from stringed instruments, which did not inspire him with horror.

To an anomalous species of terror I found him a bounden slave. 'I shall perish,' said he, 'I *must* perish in this deplorable folly. Thus, thus, and not otherwise, shall I be lost. I dread the events of the future, not in themselves, but in their results. I shudder at the thought of any, even the most trivial, incident, which may operate upon this intolerable agitation of soul. I have, indeed, no abhorrence of danger, except in its absolute effect – in terror. In this unnerved – in this pitiable condition – I feel that the period will sooner or later arrive when I must abandon life and reason together, in some struggle with the grim phantasm, FEAR.'

I learned, moreover, at intervals, and through broken and equivocal hints, another singular feature of his mental condition. He was enchained by certain superstitious impressions in regard to the dwelling which he tenanted, and whence, for many years, he had never ventured forth – in regard to an influence whose supposititious force was conveyed in terms too shadowy here to be re-stated – an influence which some peculiarities in the mere form and substance of his family mansion, had, by dint of long sufferance, he said, obtained over his spirit – an effect which the *physique* of the gray walls and turrets, and of the dim tarn into which they all looked down, had, at length, brought about upon the *morale* of his existence.

He admitted, however, although with hesitation, that much of the peculiar gloom which thus afflicted him could be traced to a more natural and far more palpable origin – to the severe and long-continued illness – indeed to the evidently approaching dissolution – of a tenderly beloved sister – his sole companion for long years – his last and only relative on earth. 'Her decease,' he said, with a bitterness which I can never forget, 'would leave him (him the hopeless and the frail) the last of the ancient race of the Ushers.' While he spoke, the lady Madeline (for so was she called) passed slowly through a remote portion of the apartment, and, without having noticed my presence, disappeared. I regarded her with an utter astonishment not unmingled with dread – and yet I found it impossible to account for such feelings. A sensation of stupor oppressed me, as my eyes followed her retreating steps. When a door, at length, closed upon her, my glance sought instinctively and eagerly the countenance of the brother – but he had buried his face in his hands, and I could only perceive that a far more than ordinary wanness had overspread the emaciated fingers through which trickled many passionate tears.

The disease of the lady Madeline had long baffled the skill of her physicians. A settled apathy, a gradual wasting away of the person, and frequent although transient affections of a partially cataleptical character, were the unusual diagnosis. Hitherto she had steadily borne up against the pressure of her malady, and had not betaken herself finally to bed; but, on the closing in of the evening of my arrival at the house, she succumbed (as her brother told me at night with inexpressible agitation) to the prostrating power of the destroyer; and I learned that the glimpse I had obtained of her person would thus probably be the last I should obtain – that the lady, at least while living, would be seen by me no more.

For several days ensuing, her name was unmentioned by either Usher or myself: and during this period I was busied in earnest endeavours to alleviate the melancholy of my friend. We painted and read together; or I listened, as if in a dream, to the wild improvisations of his speaking guitar. And thus, as a closer and still closer intimacy admitted me more unreservedly into the recesses of his spirit, the more bitterly did I perceive the futility of all attempt at cheering a mind from which darkness, as if an inherent positive quality, poured forth upon all objects of the moral and physical universe, in one unceasing radiation of gloom.

I shall ever bear about me a memory of the many solemn hours I thus spent alone with the master of the House of Usher. Yet I should fail in any attempt to convey an idea of the exact character of the studies, or of the occupations, in which he involved me, or led me the way. An excited and highly distempered ideality threw a sulphureous lustre over all. His long improvised dirges will ring forever in my ears. Among other things, I hold painfully in mind a certain singular perversion and amplification of the wild air of the last waltz of Von Weber. From the paintings over which his elaborate fancy brooded, and which grew, touch by touch, into vaguenesses at which I shuddered the more thrillingly, because I shuddered knowing not why; – from these paintings (vivid as their images now are before me) I would in vain endeavour to educe more than a small portion which should lie within the compass of merely written words. By the utter simplicity, by the nakedness of his designs, he arrested and overawed attention. If ever mortal painted an idea, that mortal was Roderick Usher. For me at least – in the circumstances then surrounding me – there arose out of the pure abstractions which the hypochondriac contrived to throw upon his canvas, an intensity of intolerable awe, no shadow of which felt I ever yet in the contemplation of the certainly glowing yet too concrete reveries of Fuseli.

One of the phantasmagoric conceptions of my friend, partaking not so rigidly of the spirit of abstraction, may be shadowed forth, although feebly, in words. A small picture presented the interior of an immensely long and rectangular vault or tunnel, with low walls, smooth, white, and without interruption or device. Certain accessory points of the design served well to convey the idea that this excavation lay at an exceeding depth below the surface of the earth. No outlet was observed in any portion of its vast extent, and no torch, or other artificial source of light was discernible; yet a flood of intense rays rolled throughout, and bathed the whole in a ghastly and inappropriate splendour.

I have just spoken of that morbid condition of the auditory nerve which rendered all music intolerable to the sufferer, with the exception of certain effects of stringed instruments. It was, perhaps, the narrow limits to which he thus confined himself upon the guitar, which gave birth, in great measure, to the fantastic character of his performances. But the fervid *facility* of his *impromptus* could not be so accounted for. They must have been, and were, in the notes, as well as in the words of his wild fantasias (for he not unfrequently accompanied himself with rhymed verbal improvisations), the result of that intense mental collectedness and concentration to which I have previously alluded as observable only in particular moments of the highest artificial excitement. The words of one of these rhapsodies I have easily remembered. I was, perhaps, the more forcibly impressed with it, as he gave it, because, in the under or mystic current of its meaning, I fancied that I perceived, and for the first time, a full consciousness on the part of Usher, of the tottering of his lofty reason upon her throne. The verses, which were entitled 'The Haunted Palace', ran very nearly, if not accurately, thus:

I

In the greenest of our valleys,
    By good angels tenanted,
Once a fair and stately palace –
    Radiant palace – reared its head.
In the monarch Thought's dominion –
    It stood there!
Never seraph spread a pinion
    Over fabric half so fair.

II

Banners yellow, glorious, golden,
    On its roof did float and flow;
(This – all this – was in the olden
    Time long ago)
And every gentle air that dallied,
    In that sweet day,
Along the ramparts plumed and pallid,
    A winged odour went away.

III

Wanderers in that happy valley
    Through two luminous windows saw
Spirits moving musically
    To a lute's well-tunèd law,
Round about a throne, where sitting
    (Porphyrogene!)
In state his glory well befitting,
    The ruler of the realm was seen.

IV

And all with pearl and ruby glowing
    Was the fair palace door,
Through which came flowing, flowing, flowing
    And sparkling evermore,

A troop of Echoes whose sweet duty
Was but to sing,
In voices of surpassing beauty,
The wit and wisdom of their king.

V

But evil things, in robes of sorrow,
Assailed the monarch's high estate;
(Ah, let us mourn, for never morrow
Shall dawn upon him, desolate!)
And, round about his home, the glory
That blushed and bloomed
Is but a dim-remembered story
Of the old time entombed.

VI

And travellers now within that valley,
Through the red-litten windows, see
Vast forms that move fantastically
To a discordant melody;
While, like a rapid ghastly river,
Through the pale door,
A hideous throng rush out forever,
And laugh – but smile no more.

I well remember that suggestions arising from this ballad, led us into a train of thought wherein there became manifest an opinion of Usher's which I mention not so much on account of its novelty, (for other men have thought thus,) as on account of the pertinacity with which he maintained it. This opinion, in its general form, was that of the sentience of all vegetable things. But, in his disordered fancy, the idea had assumed a more daring character, and trespassed, under certain conditions, upon the kingdom of inorganization. I lack words to express the full extent, or the earnest *abandon* of his persuasion. The belief, however, was connected (as I have previously hinted) with the gray stones of the home of his forefathers. The conditions of the sentience had been here, he imagined, fulfilled in the method of collocation of these stones – in the order of their arrangement, as well as in that of the many *fungi* which overspread them, and of the decayed trees which stood around – above all, in the long undisturbed endurance of this arrangement, and in its reduplication in the still waters of the tarn. Its evidence – the evidence of the sentience – was to be seen, he said, (and I here started as he spoke,) in the gradual yet certain condensation of an atmosphere of their own about the waters and the walls. The result was discoverable, he added, in that silent, yet importunate and terrible influence which for centuries had moulded the destinies of his family, and which made *him* what I now saw him – what he was. Such opinions need no comment, and I will make none.

Our books – the books which, for years, had formed no small portion of the mental existence of the invalid – were, as might be supposed, in strict keeping with this character of phantasm. We pored together over such works as the Ververt et Chartreuse of Gresset; the Belphegor of Machiavelli; the Heaven and Hell of Swedenborg; the Subterranean Voyage of Nicholas Klimm by Holberg; the Chiromancy of Robert Flud, of Jean D'Indaginé, and of De la Chambre; the Journey into the Blue Distance of Tieck; and the City of the Sun of Campanella. One favourite volume was a small octavo edition of the *Directorium Inquisitorum*, by the Dominican Eymeric de Gironne; and there were passages in Pomponius Mela, about the old African Satyrs and Ægipans, over which Usher would sit dreaming for hours. His chief delight, however, was found in the perusal of an exceedingly rare and curious book in quarto Gothic – the manual of a forgotten church – the *Vigiliæ Mortuorum secundum Chorum Ecclesiæ Maguntinæ*.

I could not help thinking of the wild ritual of this work, and of its probable influence upon the hypochondriac, when, one evening, having informed me abruptly that the lady Madeline was no more, he stated his intention of preserving her corpse for a fortnight, (previously to its final interment,) in one of the numerous vaults within the main walls of the building. The worldly reason, however, assigned for this singular proceeding, was one which I did not feel at liberty to dispute. The brother had been led to his resolution (so he told me) by consideration of the unusual character of the malady of the deceased, of certain obtrusive and eager inquiries on the part of her medical men, and of the remote and exposed situation of the burial-ground of the family. I will not deny that when I called to mind the sinister countenance of the person whom I met upon the staircase, on the day of my arrival at the house, I had no desire to oppose what I regarded as at best but a harmless, and by no means an unnatural, precaution.

At the request of Usher, I personally aided him in the arrangements for the temporary entombment. The body having been encoffined, we two alone bore it to its rest. The vault in which we placed it (and which had been so long unopened that our torches, half smothered in its oppressive atmosphere, gave us little opportunity for investigation) was small, damp, and entirely without means of admission for light; lying, at great depth, immediately beneath that portion of the building in which was my own sleeping apartment. It had been used, apparently, in remote feudal times, for the worst purposes of a donjon-keep, and, in later days, as a place of deposit for powder, or some other highly combustible substance, as a portion of its floor, and the whole interior of a long archway through which we reached it, were carefully sheathed with copper. The door, of massive iron, had been, also, similarly protected. Its immense weight caused an unusually sharp grating sound, as it moved upon its hinges.

Having deposited our mournful burden upon tressels within this region of horror, we partially turned aside the yet unscrewed lid of the coffin, and looked upon the face of the tenant. A striking similitude between the brother and sister now first arrested my attention; and Usher, divining, perhaps, my thoughts, murmured out some few words from which I learned that the deceased and himself had been twins, and that sympathies of a scarcely intelligible nature had always existed between them. Our glances, however, rested not long upon the dead – for we could not regard her unawed. The disease which had thus entombed the lady in the maturity of youth, had left, as usual in all maladies of a strictly cataleptical character, the mockery of a faint blush upon the bosom and the face, and that suspiciously lingering smile upon the lip which is so terrible in death. We replaced and screwed down the lid, and, having secured the door of iron, made our way, with toil, into the scarcely less gloomy apartments of the upper portion of the house.

And now, some days of bitter grief having elapsed, an observable change came over the features of the mental disorder of my friend. His ordinary manner had vanished. His ordinary occupations were neglected or forgotten. He roamed from chamber to chamber with hurried, unequal, and objectless step. The pallor of his countenance had assumed, if possible, a more ghastly hue – but the luminousness of his eye had utterly gone out. The once occasional huskiness of his tone was heard no more; and a tremulous quaver, as if of extreme terror, habitually characterized his utterance. There were times, indeed, when I thought his unceasingly agitated mind was labouring with some oppressive secret, to divulge which he struggled for the necessary courage. At times, again, I was obliged to resolve all into the mere inexplicable vagaries of madness, for I beheld him gazing upon vacancy for long hours, in an attitude of the profoundest attention, as if listening to some imaginary sound. It was no wonder that his condition terrified – that it infected me. I felt creeping upon me, by slow yet certain degrees, the wild influences of his own fantastic yet impressive superstitions.

It was, especially, upon retiring to bed late in the night of the seventh or eighth day after the placing of the lady Madeline within the donjon, that I experienced the full power of such feelings. Sleep came not near my couch – while the hours waned and waned away. I struggled to reason off the nervousness which had dominion over me. I endeavoured to believe that much, if not all of what I felt, was due to the bewildering influence of the gloomy furniture of the room – of the dark and tattered draperies, which, tortured into motion by the breath of a rising tempest, swayed fitfully to and fro upon the walls, and rustled uneasily about the decorations of the bed. But my efforts were fruitless. An irrepressible tremour gradually pervaded my frame; and, at length, there sat upon my very heart an incubus of utterly causeless alarm. Shaking this off with a gasp and a struggle, I uplifted myself upon the pillows, and, peering earnestly within the intense darkness of the chamber, hearkened – I know not why, except that an instinctive spirit prompted me – to certain low and indefinite sounds which came, through the pauses of the storm, at long intervals, I knew not whence. Overpowered by an intense sentiment of horror, unaccountable yet unendurable, I threw on my clothes with haste (for I felt that I should sleep no more during the night), and endeavoured to arouse myself from the pitiable condition into which I had fallen, by pacing rapidly to and fro through the apartment.

I had taken but few turns in this manner, when a light step on an adjoining staircase arrested my attention. I presently recognised it as that of Usher. In an instant afterward he rapped, with a gentle touch, at my door, and entered, bearing a lamp. His countenance was, as usual, cadaverously wan – but, moreover, there was a species of mad hilarity in his eyes – an evidently restrained *hysteria* in his whole demeanour. His air appalled me – but anything was preferable to the solitude which I had so long endured, and I even welcomed his presence as a relief.

'And you have not seen it?' he said abruptly, after having stared about him for some moments in silence – 'you have not then seen it? – but, stay! you shall.' Thus speaking, and having carefully shaded his lamp, he hurried to one of the casements, and threw it freely open to the storm.

The impetuous fury of the entering gust nearly lifted us from our feet. It was, indeed, a tempestuous yet sternly beautiful night, and one wildly singular in its terror and its beauty. A whirlwind had apparently collected its force in our vicinity; for there were frequent and violent alterations in the direction of the wind; and the exceeding density of the clouds (which hung so low as to press upon the turrets of the house) did not prevent our perceiving the life-like velocity with which they flew careering from all points against each other, without passing away into the distance. I say that even their exceeding density did not prevent our perceiving this – yet we had no glimpse of the moon or stars – nor was there any flashing forth of the lightning. But the under surfaces of the huge masses of agitated vapour, as well as all terrestrial objects immediately around us, were glowing in the unnatural light of a faintly luminous and distinctly visible gaseous exhalation which hung about and enshrouded the mansion.

'You must not – you shall not behold this!' said I, shudderingly, to Usher, as I led him, with a gentle violence, from the window to a seat. 'These appearances, which bewilder you, are merely electrical phenomena not uncommon – or it may be that they have their ghastly origin in the rank miasma of the tarn. Let us close this casement; – the air is chilling and dangerous to your frame. Here is one of your favourite romances. I will read, and you shall listen; – and so we will pass away this terrible night together.'

The antique volume which I had taken up was the 'Mad Trist' of Sir Launcelot Canning; but I had called it a favourite of Usher's more in sad jest than in earnest; for, in truth, there is little in its uncouth and unimaginative prolixity which could have had interest for the lofty and spiritual ideality of my friend. It was, however, the only book immediately at hand; and I indulged a vague hope that the excitement which now agitated the hypochondriac, might find relief (for the history of mental disorder is full of similar anomalies) even in the extremeness of the folly which I should read. Could I have judged, indeed, by the wild overstrained air of vivacity with which he hearkened, or apparently hearkened, to the words of the tale, I might well have congratulated myself upon the success of my design.

I had arrived at that well-known portion of the story where Ethelred, the hero of the Trist, having sought in vain for peaceable admission into the dwelling of the hermit, proceeds to make good an entrance by force. Here, it will be remembered, the words of the narrative run thus:

'And Ethelred, who was by nature of a doughty heart, and who was now mighty withal, on account of the powerfulness of the wine which he had drunken, waited no longer to hold parley with the hermit, who, in sooth, was of an obstinate and maliceful turn, but, feeling the rain upon his shoulders, and fearing the rising of the tempest, uplifted his mace outright, and, with blows, made quickly room in the plankings of the door for his gauntleted hand; and now pulling therewith sturdily, he so cracked, and ripped, and tore all asunder, that the noise of the dry and hollow-sounding wood alarumed and reverberated throughout the forest.'

At the termination of this sentence I started, and for a moment, paused; for it appeared to me (although I at once concluded that my excited fancy had deceived me) – it appeared to me that, from some very remote portion of the mansion, there came, indistinctly, to my ears, what might have been, in its exact similarity of character, the echo (but a stifled and dull one certainly) of the very cracking and ripping sound which Sir Launcelot had so particularly described. It was, beyond doubt, the coincidence alone which had arrested my attention; for, amid the rattling of the sashes of the casements, and the ordinary commingled noises of the still increasing storm, the sound, in itself, had nothing, surely, which should have interested or disturbed me. I continued the story:

'But the good champion Ethelred, now entering within the door, was sore enraged and amazed to perceive no signal of the maliceful hermit; but, in the stead thereof, a dragon of a scaly and prodigious demeanour, and of a fiery tongue, which sate in guard before a palace of gold, with a floor of silver; and upon the wall there hung a shield of shining brass with this legend enwritten –

> Who entereth herein, a conqueror hath bin;
> Who slayeth the dragon, the shield he shall win;

And Ethelred uplifted his mace, and struck upon the head of the dragon, which fell before him, and gave up his pesty breath, with a shriek so horrid and harsh, and withal so piercing, that Ethelred had fain to close his ears with his hands against the dreadful noise of it, the like whereof was never before heard.'

Here again I paused abruptly, and now with a feeling of wild amazement – for there could be no doubt whatever that, in this instance, I did actually hear (although from what direction it proceeded I found it impossible to say) a low and apparently distant, but harsh, protracted, and most unusual screaming or grating sound – the exact counterpart of what my fancy had already conjured up for the dragon's unnatural shriek as described by the romancer.

Oppressed, as I certainly was, upon the occurrence of the second and most extraordinary coincidence, by a thousand conflicting sensations, in which wonder and extreme terror were predominant, I still retained sufficient presence of mind to avoid exciting, by any observation, the sensitive nervousness of my companion. I was by no means certain that he had noticed the sounds in question; although, assuredly, a strange alteration had, during the last few minutes, taken place in his demeanour. From a position fronting my own, he had gradually brought round his chair, so as to sit with his face to the door of the chamber; and thus I could but partially perceive his features, although I saw that his lips trembled as if he were murmuring inaudibly. His head had dropped upon his breast – yet I knew that he was not asleep, from the wide and rigid opening of the eye as I caught a glance of it in profile. The motion of his body, too, was at variance with this idea – for he rocked from side to side with a gentle yet constant and uniform sway. Having rapidly taken notice of all this, I resumed the narrative of Sir Launcelot, which thus proceeded:

'And now, the champion, having escaped from the terrible fury of the dragon, bethinking himself of the brazen shield, and of the breaking up of the enchantment which was upon it, removed the carcass from out of the way before him, and approached valorously over the silver pavement of the castle to where the shield was upon the wall; which in sooth tarried not for his full coming, but fell down at his feet upon the silver floor, with a mighty great and terrible ringing sound.'

No sooner had these syllables passed my lips, than – as if a shield of brass had indeed, at the moment, fallen heavily upon a floor of silver – I became aware of a distinct, hollow, metallic, and clangorous, yet apparently muffled reverberation. Completely unnerved, I leaped to my feet; but the measured rocking movement of Usher was undisturbed. I rushed to the chair in which he sat. His eyes were bent fixedly before him, and throughout his whole countenance there reigned a stony rigidity. But, as I placed my hand upon his shoulder, there came a strong shudder over his whole person; a sickly smile quivered about his lips; and I saw that he spoke in a low, hurried, and gibbering murmur, as if unconscious of my presence. Bending closely over him, I at length drank in the hideous import of his words.

'Not hear it? – yes, I hear it, and *have* heard it. Long – long – long – many minutes, many hours, many days, have I heard it – yet I dared not – oh, pity me, miserable wretch that I am! – I dared not – I *dared* not speak! *We have put her living in the tomb!* Said I not that my senses were acute? I *now* tell you that I heard her first feeble movements in the hollow coffin. I heard them – many, many days ago – yet I dared not – I *dared not speak!* And now – to-night – Ethelred – ha! ha! – the breaking of the hermit's door, and the death-cry of the dragon, and the clangour of the shield! – say, rather, the rending of her coffin, and the grating of the iron hinges of her prison, and her struggles within the coppered archway of the vault! Oh whither shall I fly? Will she not be here anon? Is she not hurrying to upbraid me for my haste? Have I not heard her footstep on the stair? Do I not distinguish that heavy and horrible beating of her heart? MADMAN!' – here he sprang furiously to his feet, and shrieked out his syllables, as if in the effort he were giving up his soul – 'MADMAN! I TELL YOU THAT SHE NOW STANDS WITHOUT THE DOOR!'

As if in the superhuman energy of his utterance there had been found the potency of a spell – the huge antique panels to which the speaker pointed, threw slowly back, upon the instant, their ponderous and ebony jaws. It was the work of the rushing gust – but then without those doors there DID stand the lofty and enshrouded figure of the lady Madeline of Usher. There was blood upon her white robes, and the evidence of some bitter struggle upon every portion of her emaciated frame. For a moment she remained trembling and reeling to and fro upon the threshold, then, with a low moaning cry, fell heavily inward upon the person of her brother, and in her violent and now final death-agonies, bore him to the floor a corpse, and a victim to the terrors he had anticipated.

From that chamber, and from that mansion, I fled aghast. The storm was still abroad in all its wrath as I found myself crossing the old causeway. Suddenly there shot along the path a wild light, and I turned to see whence a gleam so unusual could have issued; for the vast house and its shadows were alone behind me. The radiance was that of the full, setting, and blood-red moon which now shone vividly through that once barely discernible fissure of which I have before spoken as extending from the roof of the building, in a zigzag direction, to the base. While I gazed, this fissure rapidly widened – there came a fierce breath of the whirlwind – the entire orb of the satellite burst at once upon my sight – my brain reeled as I saw the mighty walls rushing asunder – there was a long tumultuous shouting sound like the voice of a thousand waters – and the deep and dank tarn at my feet closed sullenly and silently over the fragments of the 'HOUSE OF USHER'.

The Cask of Amontillado

The thousand injuries of Fortunato I had borne as I best could, but when he ventured upon insult I vowed revenge. You, who so well know the nature of my soul, will not suppose, however, that I gave utterance to a threat. *At length* I would be avenged; this was a point definitely settled – but the very definitiveness with which it was resolved precluded the idea of risk. I must not only punish but punish with impunity. A wrong is unredressed when retribution overtakes its redresser. It is equally unredressed when the avenger fails to make himself felt as such to him who has done the wrong.

It must be understood that neither by word nor deed had I given Fortunato cause to doubt my good will. I continued, as was my wont, to smile in his face, and he did not perceive that my smile *now* was at the thought of his immolation.

He had a weak point – this Fortunato – although in other regards he was a man to be respected and even feared. He prided himself on his connoisseurship in wine.

Few Italians have the true virtuoso spirit. For the most part their enthusiasm is adopted to suit the time and opportunity, to practise imposture upon the British and Austrian *millionaires*. In painting and gemmary, Fortunato, like his countrymen, was a quack, but in the matter of old wines he was sincere. In this respect I did not differ from him materially; – I was skilful in the Italian vintages myself, and bought largely whenever I could.

It was about dusk, one evening during the supreme madness of the carnival season, that I encountered my friend. He accosted me with excessive warmth, for he had been drinking much. The man wore motley. He had on a tight-fitting parti-striped dress, and his head was surmounted by the conical cap and bells. I was so pleased to see him that I thought I should never have done wringing his hand.

I said to him – 'My dear Fortunato, you are luckily met. How remarkably well you are looking today. But I have received a pipe of what passes for Amontillado, and I have my doubts.'

'How?' said he. 'Amontillado? A pipe? Impossible! And in the middle of the carnival!'

'I have my doubts,' I replied; 'and I was silly enough to pay the full Amontillado price without consulting you in the matter. You were not to be found, and I was fearful of losing a bargain.'

'Amontillado!'

'I have my doubts.'

'Amontillado!'

'And I must satisfy them.'

'Amontillado!'

'As you are engaged, I am on my way to Luchresi. If any one has a critical turn it is he. He will tell me –'

'Luchresi cannot tell Amontillado from Sherry.'

'And yet some fools will have it that his taste is a match for your own.'

'Come, let us go.'

'Whither?'

'To your vaults.'

'My friend, no; I will not impose upon your good nature. I perceive you have an engagement. Luchresi –'

'I have no engagement; – come.'

'My friend, no. It is not the engagement, but the severe cold with which I perceive you are afflicted. The vaults are insufferably damp. They are encrusted with nitre.'

'Let us go, nevertheless. The cold is merely nothing. Amontillado! You have been imposed upon. And as for Luchresi, he cannot distinguish Sherry from Amontillado.'

Thus speaking, Fortunato possessed himself of my arm; and putting on a mask of black silk and drawing a *roquelaire* closely about my person, I suffered him to hurry me to my palazzo.

There were no attendants at home; they had absconded to make merry in honour of the time. I had told them that I should not return until the morning, and had given them explicit orders not to stir from the house. These orders were sufficient, I well knew, to insure their immediate disappearance, one and all, as soon as my back was turned.

I took from their sconces two flambeaux, and giving one to Fortunato, bowed him through several suites of rooms to the archway that led into the vaults. I passed down a long and winding staircase, requesting him to be cautious as he followed. We came at length to the foot of the descent, and stood together upon the damp ground of the catacombs of the Montresors.

The gait of my friend was unsteady, and the bells upon his cap jingled as he strode.

'The pipe,' he said.

'It is farther on,' said I; 'but observe the white web-work which gleams from these cavern walls.'

He turned towards me, and looked into my eyes with two filmy orbs that distilled the rheum of intoxication.

'Nitre?' he asked, at length.

'Nitre,' I replied. 'How long have you had that cough?'

'Ugh! ugh! ugh! – ugh! ugh! ugh! – ugh! ugh! ugh! – ugh! ugh! ugh! – ugh! ugh! ugh!'

My poor friend found it impossible to reply for many minutes.

'It is nothing,' he said, at last.

'Come,' I said, with decision, 'we will go back; your health is precious. You are rich, respected, admired, beloved; you are happy, as once I was. You are a man to be missed. For me it is no matter. We will go back; you will be ill, and I cannot be responsible. Besides, there is Luchresi –'

'Enough,' he said; 'the cough is a mere nothing; it will not kill me. I shall not die of a cough.'

'True – true,' I replied; 'and, indeed, I had no intention of alarming you unnecessarily – but you should use all proper caution. A draught of this Medoc will defend us from the damps.'

Here I knocked off the neck of a bottle which I drew from a long row of its fellows that lay upon the mould.

'Drink,' I said, presenting him the wine.

He raised it to his lips with a leer. He paused and nodded to me familiarly, while his bells jingled.

'I drink,' he said, 'to the buried that repose around us.'

'And I to your long life.'

He again took my arm, and we proceeded.

'These vaults,' he said, 'are extensive.'

'The Montresors,' I replied, 'were a great and numerous family.'

'I forget your arms.'

'A huge human foot d'or, in a field azure; the foot crushes a serpent rampant whose fangs are imbedded in the heel.'

'And the motto?'

'*Nemo me impune lacessit.*'

'Good!' he said.

The wine sparkled in his eyes and the bells jingled. My

own fancy grew warm with the Medoc. We had passed through long walls of piled skeletons, with casks and puncheons intermingling, into the inmost recesses of the catacombs. I paused again, and this time I made bold to seize Fortunato by an arm above the elbow.

'The nitre!' I said; 'see, it increases. It hangs like moss upon the vaults. We are below the river's bed. The drops of moisture trickle among the bones. Come, we will go back ere it is too late. Your cough –'

'It is nothing,' he said; 'let us go on. But first, another draught of the Medoc.'

I broke and reached him a flagon of De Grâve. He emptied it at a breath. His eyes flashed with a fierce light. He laughed and threw the bottle upwards with a gesticulation I did not understand.

I looked at him in surprise. He repeated the movement – a grotesque one.

'You do not comprehend?' he said.

'Not I,' I replied.

'Then you are not of the brotherhood.'

'How?'

'You are not of the masons.'

'Yes, yes,' I said; 'yes, yes.'

'You? Impossible! A mason?'

'A mason,' I replied.

'A sign,' he said, 'a sign.'

'It is this,' I answered, producing from beneath the folds of my *roquelaire* a trowel.

'You jest,' he exclaimed, recoiling a few paces. 'But let us proceed to the Amontillado.'

'Be it so,' I said, replacing the tool beneath the cloak and again offering him my arm. He leaned upon it heavily. We continued our route in search of the Amontillado. We passed through a range of low arches, descended, passed on, and descending again, arrived at a deep crypt, in which the foulness of the air caused our flambeaux rather to glow than flame.

At the most remote end of the crypt there appeared another less spacious. Its walls had been lined with human remains, piled to the vault overhead, in the fashion of the great catacombs of Paris. Three sides of this interior crypt were still ornamented in this manner. From the fourth side the bones had been thrown down, and lay promiscuously upon the earth, forming at one point a mound of some size. Within the wall thus exposed by the displacing of the bones, we perceived a still interior crypt or recess, in depth about four feet, in width three, in height six or seven. It seemed to have been constructed for no especial use within itself, but formed merely the interval between two of the colossal supports of the roof of the catacombs, and was backed by one of their circumscribing walls of solid granite.

It was in vain that Fortunato, uplifting his dull torch, endeavoured to pry into the depth of the recess. Its termination the feeble light did not enable us to see.

'Proceed,' I said; 'herein is the Amontillado. As for Luchresi –'

'He is an ignoramus,' interrupted my friend, as he stepped unsteadily forward, while I followed immediately at his heels. In an instant he had reached the extremity of the niche, and finding his progress arrested by the rock, stood stupidly bewildered. A moment more and I had fettered him to the granite. In its surface were two iron staples, distant from each other about two feet, horizontally. From one of these depended a short chain, from the other a padlock. Throwing the links about his waist, it was but the work of a few seconds to secure it. He was too much astounded to resist. Withdrawing the key I stepped back from the recess.

'Pass your hand,' I said, 'over the wall; you cannot help feeling the nitre. Indeed, it is *very* damp. Once more let me *implore* you to return. No? Then I must positively leave you. But I must first render you all the little attentions in my power.'

'The Amontillado!' ejaculated my friend, not yet recovered from his astonishment.

'True,' I replied; 'the Amontillado.'

As I said these words I busied myself among the pile of bones of which I have before spoken. Throwing them aside, I soon uncovered a quantity of building stone and mortar. With these materials and with the aid of my trowel, I began vigorously to wall up the entrance of the niche.

I had scarcely laid the first tier of the masonry when I discovered that the intoxication of Fortunato had in a great measure worn off. The earliest indication I had of this was a low moaning cry from the depth of the recess. It was *not* the cry of a drunken man. There was then a long and obstinate silence. I laid the second tier, and the third, and the fourth; and then I heard the furious vibrations of the chain. The noise lasted for several minutes, during which, that I might hearken to it with the more satisfaction, I ceased my labours and sat down upon the bones. When at last the clanking subsided, I resumed the trowel, and finished without interruption the fifth, the sixth, and the seventh tier. The wall was now nearly upon a level with my breast. I again paused, and holding the flambeaux over the mason-work, threw a few feeble rays upon the figure within.

A succession of loud and shrill screams, bursting suddenly from the throat of the chained form, seemed to thrust me violently back. For a brief moment I hesitated, I trembled. Unsheathing my rapier, I began to grope with it about the recess; but the thought of an instant reassured me. I placed my hand upon the solid fabric of the catacombs, and felt satisfied. I re-approached the wall; I replied to the yells of him who clamoured. I re-echoed, I aided, I surpassed them in volume and in strength. I did this, and the clamourer grew still.

It was now midnight, and my task was drawing to a

close. I had completed the eighth, the ninth and the tenth tier. I had finished a portion of the last and the eleventh; there remained but a single stone to be fitted and plastered in. I struggled with its weight; I placed it partially in its destined position. But now there came from out the niche a low laugh that erected the hairs upon my head. It was succeeded by a sad voice, which I had difficulty in recognizing as that of the noble Fortunato. The voice said –

'Ha! ha! ha! – he! he! he! – a very good joke, indeed – an excellent jest. We will have many a rich laugh about it at the palazzo – he! he! he! – over our wine – he! he! he!'

'The Amontillado!' I said.

'He! he! he! – he! he! he! – yes, the Amontillado. But is it not getting late? Will not they be awaiting us at the palazzo, the Lady Fortunato and the rest? Let us be gone.'

'Yes,' I said, 'let us be gone.'

'*For the love of God, Montresor!*'

'Yes,' I said, 'for the love of God!'

But to these words I hearkened in vain for a reply. I grew impatient. I called aloud –

'Fortunato!'

No answer. I called again –

'Fortunato!'

No answer still. I thrust a torch through the remaining aperture and let it fall within. There came forth in return only a jingling of the bells. My heart grew sick; it was the dampness of the catacombs that made it so. I hastened to make an end of my labour. I forced the last stone into its position; I plastered it up. Against the new masonry I re-erected the old rampart of bones. For the half of a century no mortal has disturbed them. *In pace requiescat!*

PENGUIN

LITTLE BLACK

CLASSICS

“不多久我听到了一声
轻微的呻吟，我知道
这是人在极度恐惧下
发出的呻吟……
从灵魂深处发出的
低沉而压抑的声音……”

PENGUIN

LITTLE BLACK

CLASSICS

泄密的心

The Tell-Tale Heart

[美] 爱伦 · 坡 著

马爱农 译

中信出版集团 · 北京

图书在版编目（CIP）数据

企鹅经典·小黑书.第一辑:英、汉/(日)吉田兼好等著;文东等译.-- 北京:中信出版社,2018.11(2022.7 重印)

书名原文:Penguin Little Black Classics

ISBN 978-7-5086-9400-9

Ⅰ.①企… Ⅱ.①吉… ②文… Ⅲ.①世界文学一作品综合集一英、汉 Ⅳ.①I11

中国版本图书馆 CIP 数据核字 (2018) 第 193780 号

The Tell Tale Heart
'The Fall of the House of Usher' was first published in 1839, 'The Tell-Tale Heart' in 1843, and 'The Cask of Amontillado' in 1846. This selection published in Penguin Classics 2015. The moral right of the translator has been asserted. Simplified Chinese translation copyright © 马爱农. All rights reserved.

本书仅限中国大陆地区发行销售

®“企鹅”及其相关标识是企鹅图书有限公司已经注册或尚未注册的商标。
未经允许，不得擅用。
封底凡无企鹅防伪标识者均属未经授权之非法版本。

企鹅经典：小黑书　第一辑

泄密的心

著　　者：[美]爱伦·坡
译　　者：马爱农
出版发行：中信出版集团股份有限公司
（北京市朝阳区惠新东街甲 4 号富盛大厦 2 座 邮编 100029）
承 印 者：河北鹏润印刷有限公司

开　　本：787mm×1092mm　1/32　　印　　张：41　　字　　数：300 千字
版　　次：2018 年 11 月第 1 版　　印　　次：2022 年 7 月第13次印刷
京权图字：01-2018-6477
书　　号：ISBN 978-7-5086-9400-9
定　　价：149.00 元（全 10 册）

版权所有·侵权必究
如有印刷、装订问题，本公司负责调换。

服务热线：400-600-8099
投稿邮箱：author@citicpub.com

目录

泄密的心

对！神经质，我一直都患有严重的神经质；但是你们为什么要说我疯了呢？我的病并没有摧毁我的感觉力，没有使它变得迟钝，而是使它更加敏锐。尤其是听力异常地敏锐。我听得到天上和地下的所有声音。我听到地狱里的许多事情。试想，我怎么会是疯子呢？听吧！我来给你们把事情的来龙去脉讲一讲，看我讲得多么有条有理，心平气和。

不知道这个念头是什么时候钻进我的脑子里的；可是一旦形成，它就没日没夜地缠着我。说起来没有任何目的，也没有任何冲动的情感。我喜欢那个老头儿。他从来没有亏待过我，从来没有侮辱过我。我也不贪图他

的财富。我想是他的眼睛！对，就是这个！他有一只眼睛很像兀鹰的眼——一只浅蓝色的，上面蒙着一层薄翳的眼睛。每当这目光一落到我身上，我浑身的血液就变得冰凉；因此我渐渐地很慢很慢地下定了决心，要干掉那个老头儿，从而永远摆脱那只眼睛。

要害就在这里。你们以为我疯了。疯子什么都不知道。可是你们没看到我是怎么做的。你们没看到我干得多么漂亮！那样地小心谨慎、深谋远虑，那样巧妙地掩饰！在下手的前一个星期中，我对老头儿比什么时候都好。每晚午夜时分，我悄悄拨动他的门闩，推开门——哦，动作轻极了！然后，当门缝打开到我的头可以伸进去的时候，我先把一只黑灯笼塞进去，灯笼上下封得严严实实，没有一丝光线漏出，然后我把脑袋伸了进去。哦，你要是看到我当时的那个机灵样，一定会哈哈大笑的！我的动作很慢，慢极了，生怕把老头儿从睡梦中惊醒。我用了一个钟头的时间才把整个脑袋伸进门缝，使我能看到他躺在床上。哈！——一个疯子会这样聪明吗？然后，当我的头完全伸进屋里之后，我小心地打开灯笼——哦，那么小心——小心（因为铰链会吱呀作响）。只打开那么一点，让一丝细细的光线落在那只兀鹰般的

眼睛上。就这样我一连去了七个晚上，每次都在午夜时分，可是那只眼睛总是闭着的，这样我就无法干那桩事。因为惹恼我的并不是那个老头儿，而是他邪恶的眼睛。每天早晨天一亮，我就大胆地走进他的房间，勇敢地和他攀谈，亲热地唤着他的名字，问他晚上睡得可好。所以你瞧，老头儿要能想到我在每天午夜时分趁他睡着的时候窥视他的话，那他可真是老谋深算了。

第八个晚上我开门的时候特别地小心。手表的分针都比我的手动得快些。那晚我第一次感觉到了自己的力量有多大，感觉到自己是多么聪明。我几乎无法控制自己的得意。想想吧，我在那儿一点点地推门，而他做梦都想不到我秘密的行动和思想。想到这里我不禁窃笑了起来；可能听到了我的声音，床上的他突然动了一下，像是受了惊。你可能以为我会退缩——可我没有。他的房间漆黑一片，伸手不见五指（百叶窗紧紧地关着，因为怕有强盗），我知道他不会看见门开了，所以我继续稳稳地、稳稳地推动房门。

我把头伸进来了，正要打开灯笼时，我的手指不小心碰动了洋铁闩，老头儿从床上腾地坐了起来，叫道："谁在那儿？"

我不吱声，一动不动地站着。整整一小时我一块肌肉都没动一下，同时也没有听到他躺下。他仍旧坐在床上听着；就像我自己这样，整夜整夜地，听着墙中死神守望者的声音。

不多久我听到了一声轻微的呻吟，我知道这是人在极度恐惧下发出的呻吟。它不是疼痛或悲哀的呻吟。哦，不是的！它是在不堪恐惧的重压时，从灵魂深处发出的低沉而压抑的声音。我很熟悉这种声音。许多夜晚，午夜时分，全世界都在熟睡的时候，它也会从我自己的胸中涌出，带着可怕的回音，加深了那令我不安的恐惧。我说我很了解。我了解老头儿的感受，并同情他，尽管我在心里偷偷暗笑。我知道自从听到第一声微响，他在床上翻了个身以后，他就一直没有再睡着。他的恐惧在不断地增强。他试图想象它们是毫无根据的，可是不能够。他对自己说“那只是烟囱里的风，那只是一只耗子跑过去了”或“只不过是一只蟋蟀叫了一声”。是的，他试图用这些假设来安慰自己，可是都没有用，都没用，因为死神在悄悄走近他时，已经把自己的影子投在了他的身上，把他整个笼罩了。正是这无形的影子的悲惨影响使他感到了——尽管他既没有看到也没有听到——房

间中我的脑袋的存在。

我非常耐心地等了很长的时间，还没有听到他躺下，于是我决定把灯笼打开一条缝，一丝极小极小的缝。我便这么做了，你想象不出我是多么小心翼翼，小心翼翼，终于，缝隙中射出一线微光，细若蛛丝，正好落在那只兀鹰般的眼睛上。

那眼睛睁着，大大地睁着，我凝视着它，不禁火冒三丈。我对它看得一清二楚，灰暗的蓝眼珠，上面还蒙着一层可恶的薄翳，它使我骨髓发凉；可是我看不到老头儿脸上或身体的其他任何部分，我好像是本能地把光线对准了那个该死的部位。

我不是说过被你们当作疯子的人只是感觉过于敏锐吗？现在，啊，我听到了一种低低的、沉闷而急促的声音，像是一只裹在棉花里的表在响。我对这声音也很熟悉。这是那老头儿的心跳。它加剧着我的愤怒，就像战鼓激发士兵的勇气一样。即使是这样我仍然克制住了自己，静悄悄地站着，几乎连气都不出。我一动不动地举着灯笼，看自己能使光线在那只眼睛上保持得多稳。与此同时，那可怕的咚咚的心跳声在加剧，它每时每刻越来越快，越来越响。老头儿一定恐惧到了极点！它越来

越响，随着时间的推移，一刻响过一刻！你听仔细了吗？我告诉过你我有些神经质，我确实是这样。半夜三更，在那座静得可怕的老房子里，这样一种奇怪的声音使我产生了无法控制的恐惧。然而，我克制着自己又待了几分钟没有动。可是那心跳越来越响，越来越响！我觉得那颗心要爆炸了。这时一种新的焦虑攫住了我，这声音会被邻居听到的！老头儿的死期到了！我一声大叫，扯开灯笼，跳进屋内。他尖叫一声，只一声。转眼我已把他拖到地上，拖过沉重的被褥压在他身上。然后我开心地微笑起来，这桩事情干完了。可是，那颗心继续沉闷地跳动了许多分钟。不过我并不为此而烦恼，隔着墙，人们是不会听到的。最后它终于停止了。老头儿死了。我搬开被子对尸体进行检查。没错，他已经死得跟石头一样了。我把手在他的心口上放了许久。没有搏动，他死得和石头一样了。他的眼睛再也不会使我心烦了。

如果你认为我疯了，那么等我讲述了我藏匿尸体时的谨慎周全之后，你就不会再这么想了。黑夜在渐渐过去，我急促却无声无息地干着活。首先我把尸体肢解了，把脑袋、胳膊和腿切了下来。

接着我抽出了三块地板，把尸体全部塞入地板中间，

然后把地板重新铺好，铺得那样聪明，那样巧妙，任凭谁的眼睛——就连他的眼睛——也看不出任何破绽。没有什么需要冲洗，没有任何污迹，半点血迹也没有。我非常机警，全部都接在一只盆里了——哈！哈！

当我干完时，约莫是四点钟的光景，天仍然黑得像半夜一样。正在钟打四点的时候，大门上响起了敲门声。我怀着一颗轻松的心去开门，现在我有什么可怕的呢？进来了三个男人，十分和蔼地自我介绍说他们是警官。一个邻居在夜里听到了一声尖叫，因疑心有不轨行为，向警察局报了案，他们（这三个警官）奉命对屋子进行搜查。

我笑了，我有什么可怕的？我欢迎三位先生的来访。我说那声尖叫是我自己在睡梦中发出的。我提到那老头儿去乡下了。我领着客人视察了整幢房子。我请他们仔细地搜查。最后我把他们带到了他的房间。我让他们看他的财宝，样样安好，纹丝未动。我仗着自信头脑一热，干脆搬来了几把椅子，让他们就在这里歇一歇脚。我得意忘形，把自己的椅子正好搁在了安放死者尸体的那个地方。

警官很满意。我的态度打消了他们的疑心。我泰然

自若。他们坐在那儿，我愉快地回答他们的问题，于是他们随便地闲聊起来。可是，没过多久，我感到自己脸色开始发白，希望他们快走。我的头疼了起来，耳朵里有个声音在响，可他们还坐在那里聊着。耳朵里的声音清晰起来了，它继续响着，越来越清晰。我更起劲地说话，试图摆脱这种感觉；可是它仍然在响，而且更清晰了，直到最后，我发现那声音不是在我的耳朵里。

我的脸色现在一定非常苍白，可是我更流利地说话，并且提高了嗓门儿。然而那声音更响了，我能怎么办呢？那是一种低低的、沉闷而急促的声音，很像一只裹在棉花里的表发出的声音。我喘息着，然而警官们没听到它。我更快地说话，我更激烈地说话；可那声音在不断地增强。我站起来，打着激烈的手势，提高了调门为一些小事而争论，可那声音在不断地增强。他们为什么还不走？我迈着沉重的步子在地板上走来走去，仿佛被他们的话所激怒，可那声音在不断地增强。哦，上帝啊！我能怎么办呢？我口吐白沫，我胡言乱语，我发誓赌咒！我挥舞着我坐的那把椅子，把它在地板上碾动，可是那声音高过了这一切，而且不断地增强着。它越来越响，越来越响，越来越响！那几个人仍然愉快地聊着，

而且微笑着。他们会不会没有听见？万能的上帝！——不，不可能！他们听到了！——他们怀疑了！——他们知道了！——他们在讥笑着我的恐惧！——我这样想，现在也还这样想。可是什么都比这种痛苦要强！什么都比这种嘲笑要好受些！我再也受不了这种虚伪的微笑了！我感到必须要大声尖叫，或者死掉！——来来——又来了！——听啊！越来越响！越来越响！越来越响！越来越响！——

“坏家伙们！”我尖叫道，“别装了！我招认！——扯开地板！——这儿，就是这儿！——是他那颗该死的心在跳！”

厄歇尔府的倒塌

你的心是敏感的弦琴，轻轻一触便发出幽鸣。

——德·贝朗热

那年秋季的一天，整个白天愁云惨雾，死气沉沉，听不见一点声音，黑压压的乌云低悬在空中。我独自骑着马，穿过一片特别阴郁肃杀的乡村，最后当黄昏渐至，夜幕四合的时候，终于看见了那座忧郁的厄歇尔府邸。我不知道究竟是怎么回事，但当我第一眼看见那所房子，就有一种感伤之情在我心头弥漫，令我无法忍受。我说无法忍受，是因为当人们目睹自然界最荒凉萧条、最阴沉恐怖的景象时，通常会产生一种因富有诗意而令人欣

慰的情愫，而此刻我的感伤却没有因这种情愫而得到丝毫解脱。我凝望眼前的这幅景象，凝望那座孤零零的房屋，以及周围纯朴的地貌风景，凝望那惨白凄凉的墙壁，凝望那像眼睛一样惆怅失神的窗户，凝望那几排熏衣草，凝望那几棵枯树的白色树干，内心感到万念俱灰，我只能把这种心境比作瘾君子服用鸦片后大梦初醒、陷入庸常生活后的痛苦以及脱去伪装面纱时的恐惧，除此之外没有任何尘世的情怀所能比拟。这是一种冷彻骨髓的感觉，是一种越陷越深的感觉，是一种心灵深处的厌憎，是一种从未体验过的恐怖意识，无论怎样百般地刺激想象力，都无法体会到任何崇高之感。是什么——我凝神静思——是什么使得我在凝视厄歇尔府邸时感到如此忧郁惆怅？这是一个无法破解的谜。而且我在沉思时无法抓住那些逼近我的阴暗朦胧的幻觉。我不得不勉强地聊以自慰地这么判定：肯定是一些十分简单的自然物体结合在一起，对我们构成了如此强烈的震撼力，而对这种力量的分析则超出了我们的理解深度。我思忖道，只要把这幅景象中的特殊物体稍做调整，把画面的细节略加修改，就足以改变甚至消灭它那令人无限忧伤的特性。为了把我的这一思想付诸实施，我勒住缰绳使马慢下步

子，来到一个漆黑可怖的山中小湖的陡峭岸边。这个小湖坐落在寓所旁边，闪耀着宁静的光泽。我朝下面望去，却猛地打了一个寒噤，我看到灰色熏衣草、模样狰狞的树干和眼睛般空洞的窗户在水中扭曲的倒影，比刚才更感到毛骨悚然。

尽管如此，我还是建议自己在这座阴郁的房子里逗留几个星期。房子的主人罗德里克·厄歇尔曾经是我儿童时代的一个玩伴，但是我们已经有许多年没有见面了。不过，最近他有一封信寄给千里迢迢之外的我，其中以迫切的、不近情理的口吻，叫我务必亲自给他答复。信的手稿显示他的心情焦虑不安。写信人说到严重的身体疾病，说到一种令他忧虑的精神失常，还说到想见我一面的迫切愿望，因为我是他最亲，实际上也是唯一知心的朋友，他希望通过和我轻松愉快的交往，能够多少减轻他的疾病。他就是用这种口吻说到这些和其他许多事情的，他显然是以一片真心向我提出请求的，不允许我有半点迟疑。于是，我立刻服从了这一我仍然认为非常蹊跷的召唤。

尽管我们童年时代是十分亲密的玩伴，其实我对这位朋友了解甚少。他一向不爱说话，沉默寡言是他的习

惯。不过，我知道他的渊源悠久的家族，多年以来一直因性情极为敏感而闻名。在久远的过去，这种敏感曾经通过许多杰出的艺术作品得到展现，而最近，这种敏感又通过不断慷慨而又谦逊的乐善好施得到体现，此外还有对复杂的音乐科学的全身心的热爱，这甚至超过对传统的、一目了然的美的恋慕。我还了解到这样一个惊人的事实，厄歇尔家族尽管多少年来深孚众望，但其根基上从未生长出常青不朽的枝蔓。也就是说，整个家庭代代一脉单传，除了十分个别、十分暂时的例外，总是人丁不旺。我一边思绪如潮地想着这座府邸的特色与厄歇尔的家族特征完全相符，想着在多少个漫长的世纪里，房屋可能对人产生的影响，同时想到，就是这种不足，这种也许属于次要问题的缺憾，以及由此产生的父亲将遗产和姓氏不偏不倚地传给儿子的做法，最终使得两者合而为一，把房屋原来的名字变成了“厄歇尔府”这个古怪而双关的称呼。这一称呼在使用它的庄户人看来，似乎既包含家族，又包含着家族宅屋的意思。

前面已经说过，我那多少有点孩子气的试验——在山中小湖边俯瞰——的唯一结果反倒是加深了最初的那种奇特印象。毫无疑问，我越是意识到迷信思想——为

什么不能用这个词呢？——在我心中迅速泛滥，越是反而加速了它的泛滥。这就是基于恐怖的一切情感的荒谬法则，我很久以前就知道。也许正是仅仅由于这个原因，当我再次将目光从水中倒影中抬起，转而凝望宅屋本身时，心里便产生了一种奇特的幻想，这幻想是如此荒诞不经，我之所以提到它，只是为了说明当时困扰我的情感是多么鲜明强烈。我努力调动我的想象力，使自己真的相信，在这整个宅屋和领地上，笼罩着一种它们及毗邻地区所特有的气氛，这种气氛和空中的大气没有任何相似之处，它是从枯朽的古树、灰暗的墙壁和寂寞的小湖中散发出来的，是一种瘟疫般有害的、神秘诡谲的雾气，沉闷，迟滞，若隐若现，是一种沉甸甸的铅灰色。

我摆脱精神上那种如梦似幻的感觉，更加专注地审视那座宅屋的真实面貌。它最主要的特点似乎就在于极其古老。无数个岁月的风吹日晒使它剥蚀褪色。房子外部长满细小的菌类，像错综复杂的网一样，从屋檐上悬挂下来。然而，这一切绝不能算特别破败凋敝。砖石结构的每一部分都完好无损，它各个部分依然十分协调，但每块石头已渐渐碎裂，这之间似乎存在某种狂乱的、自相矛盾的东西。这不由得使我想起华而不实的老式木

结构建筑：在漫长的岁月里，某个被人忽视的拱顶由于长年不通风，正在渐渐腐烂。不过，这座房屋除了外表有大面积的破败以外，整体结构丝毫没有动摇欲坠之感。也许，某个一丝不苟的观察者会发现一道几乎不易察觉的裂缝，从正面的屋顶延伸下来，蜿蜒曲折地贯穿整个墙壁，最后隐入小湖的死水中。

我注意到了这些，便骑马穿过一条短短的堤道，来到宅屋前。一位等在那里的仆人把马接了过去，我则跨入门厅哥特式的拱廊。一个男仆迈着鬼鬼祟祟的步子，一言不发地领我穿过许多黑暗而曲折的甬道，来到他主人的书房。不知怎的，一路上目之所及，竟使我刚才描述过的那种无法言说的感觉更加强烈了。尽管周围的一切——天花板上的雕画、墙壁上阴暗的挂毯、漆黑的乌木地板，以及随着我的脚步嗒嗒作响、显得鬼影幢幢的盔甲纪念品，都只是，或类似于我童年时代就已然看惯的事物——尽管迟疑着不愿意承认我对这一切是多么熟悉，我依然惊异地发现一些普通的形象竟能在人心里激起如此陌生的幻想。在一道楼梯上，我遇见了这里的家庭医生。在我看来，他的脸上是一种夹杂着卑劣狡诈和困惑茫然的混合表情。他惊惶失措地向我打个招呼，与

我擦肩而过。这时男仆猛地推开一扇门，示意我进去见他的主人。

进到里面，我发现这是一个非常宽敞和高大的房间。窗户又长又窄，棱角分明，而且高高地远离乌黑的栎木地板，人在房间里根本接触不到它们。透过格子结构的窗玻璃，照射进几缕微弱的深红色的光线，使得周围几件比较突出的物体清晰可见；然而，若竭力想要看清房间里最深远的角落，或拱形的回纹饰天花板的幽秘之处，则是白费气力。墙壁上挂着黑暗的装饰布。整个房间布置铺张奢侈，古色古香，却毫无舒适之感，而且已是破旧不堪。到处散乱地放着许多书籍和乐器，却没有使整个房间增添丝毫活力。我感到自己呼吸到的是一种忧伤的气息。到处都笼罩着、弥漫着一种冷峻、幽深、无法改变的阴郁气氛。

看到我进来，厄歇尔从他平躺着的沙发上站起身来，以一种兴高采烈的热情招呼我。我起初认为，这种热情中包含着许多做过了头的亲热劲儿——是一个厌世者在强颜欢笑。但是，当我一眼瞥见他的面容时，才相信他的热情完全发自内心。我们坐了下来，他有片刻没有说话，我便带着一种半是怜悯半是惊惧的心情凝视着他。

确实，从未见过有人像罗德里克·厄歇尔这样，在如此短的时间内，产生了如此触目惊心的变化！我好不容易才强迫自己承认，眼前的这个男人就是我孩提时代的玩伴。不过，他的面部特征倒一直都很鲜明独特。他脸如死灰，大大的眼睛泪汪汪的，放射出无与伦比的光芒；嘴唇略微薄了一点，没有一丝血色，但曲线轮廓却精美绝伦；鼻子是典雅的希伯来式，但鼻孔极为宽大，这在类似的鼻形中是十分少见的；下巴线条精致，轮廓并不突出，这说明了他在精神上缺少活力；头发柔软、纤细，酷似蛛网。这些面部特征，再加上天庭极为饱满宽阔，使他的模样令人难以忘怀。此刻，他的面部特征和一贯流露的神情，只比过去略微显著一些，却使他产生了如此惊人的变化，我简直怀疑是不是在跟他说话。最令我震惊甚至恐惧的，是他此刻死一般惨白的脸色，和他此刻眼睛里放射出的奇异的光芒。柔软如丝般的头发，主人无暇以顾，任其杂乱无章地生长着，丝丝缕缕的细发不是垂落下来，而是在面颊上随意流淌，我尽管拼命努力，也无法把这种奇异的面部表情与正常的人的概念联系起来。

我立刻就注意到我这位朋友的一举一动都颠三倒四，

很不协调；很快，我发现这是由于他在吃力地克制一种惯性的痉挛——一种极度的神经焦虑，却又怎么也克制不住。对他的这副模样，我倒是有心理准备，一是因为读了他的来信，二是因为对他童年时的某些特征记忆犹新，三是因为从他与众不同的体质和脾性可以得出这样的结论。他的动作一会儿充满生机，一会儿垂头丧气。他的声音也瞬息多变，忽而吞吞吐吐、闪烁其辞（这时他身体里的元气似乎一时荡然无存），忽而又干脆有力、斩钉截铁——嗓音果断、沉着，掷地有声，听起来似乎不太真实，那种沉稳、镇定、被运用得游刃有余的喉音，只有神志恍惚的醉鬼，或是不可救药的烟鬼在极度兴奋、神魂颠倒时，才能发得出来。

他就是用这种口吻谈到他邀我前来的目的，说他诚心地盼着我，希望我给他提供安慰。他还颇为细致地谈到他自认为他的病情属于何种性质。他说，那是一种先天性的家族遗传病，他对药物治疗已经不抱任何希望。接着他又补充说道，这只是一种神经性疾病，不久自会痊愈。该病的症状是他经常出现大量离奇古怪的感觉。他详细叙述这些感觉，其中一些令我既感到有趣，又感到疑惑，尽管这也许是他说话时的措辞和口气在起作用。

一种病态的神经过敏使他备受折磨；他只能吃最寡淡无味的饭菜；只能穿某一种面料的衣服；所有鲜花的芬芳都令他窒息；他的眼睛即使在微弱的光线下也刺痛难忍；而且，只有一些特殊的声音和弦乐器奏出的音响，他听了才不会感到心惊胆寒。

我看出来，他完全陷于变态的恐惧中不能自拔。“我要死了，”他说，“我一定会在这可悲的疯狂感觉中送命。就那样，就那样死去，不会有别的出路。我对将来要发生的事情感到害怕，倒不是害怕这些事情本身，而是害怕它们带来的后果。一想到任何意外，哪怕是最微不足道的小事，都会令我这敏感焦虑的心灵受到震撼，我就感到不寒而栗。说实在的，我倒不怕灾祸，怕就怕灾祸带来的绝对后果，它使我胆战心惊。在这种惶惶不可终日的状态下，在这种凄惨可悲的处境下，我感到那个时刻迟早都会到来，我定会在与恐惧这个狰狞幻影的一次抗争中，彻底放弃我的生命和理智。”

此外，我还不时从他那吞吞吐吐、含义模糊的暗示中，发现了他精神状态的另一个奇怪特征。他内心纠缠着许多迷信想法，都是关于他多年居住、从不敢擅自离开的那幢府邸——关于一种影响力，而他在谈到他所

想象的这种影响力的能量时用词晦涩，使我在此无法复述——他说，由于常年忍受这幢府邸的形状实质上的某些特异之处，使他的精神受到了某种影响，那灰墙、塔楼，以及它们倒映其中的那一湖幽暗的死水，这所有的景象最终对他的生存状态产生了一种影响。

不过，他虽然犹疑再三，还是承认说，这种令他痛不欲生的异样的忧郁情绪，多半可以追溯到某个更合乎情理、更明白显见的根源。那是因为他心爱的妹妹，他多少年来唯一的伴侣，他在世上仅存的亲人，长时间来一直重病缠身，实际上已经眼看着奄奄一息了。“她一旦死去，”他说道，那口气里的酸楚令我难以忘怀，“这古老的厄歇尔家族就剩下我一个人（一个孤苦无望、精神脆弱的人）。”他正说着，玛德琳小姐（别人就是这样称呼她的）从房间的尽头慢慢走过，根本没有留意我的存在，就兀自隐去了。我凝视着她，突然产生一种极度的惊诧，甚至还夹杂着一些恐惧。但是要解释这种感觉所为何来，我却不能办到。我的目光追随着她离去的背影，心里感到一阵恍惚。最后，房门在她身后关上，我不由自主、迫不及待地转眼去看她哥哥的神情，然而他已用双手将脸紧紧捂住，我只能看见他那瘦骨嶙峋的手指显

得比平时更加苍白，一行行冲动的泪水从指缝间滚落。

玛德琳小姐的病早就使那些医生束手无策。不可改变的冷漠倦怠，日渐消瘦的身体，再加上尽管转瞬即逝，却时常都要发作的强直性昏厥症，这些便是她的种种反常症候。她一直顽强地同病魔抗争，始终不甘心就此一病不起。但在我到达这里的当天晚上夜色渐浓时（她的哥哥在夜里失魂落魄地告诉我），她最终屈从于死神的淫威。我这才知道，我目送她背影的那匆匆一瞥，也许就是我见到她的最后一眼——那位小姐，至少在她弥留的时候，我是不会再见到她了。

在随后的几天里，厄歇尔和我都绝口不提她的名字。在此期间，我一直真心诚意地想法减轻我朋友的伤悲。我们一起绘画，一起读书，或者我就聆听他即兴弹奏他那把如泣如诉的吉他，宛若在梦境一般。这种朝夕相处，使我们越来越亲密，也使我越来越深入地了解他的内心世界，使我越来越痛苦地看出无论我怎样千方百计地鼓励他振作起来、摆脱忧郁，都是枉费心机，毫无结果。仿佛有一种与生俱来、根深蒂固的痛苦，像一道不死的幽光一样，把他精神世界和物质世界的一切笼罩得一片昏暗。

我就这样独自陪伴厄歇尔府的主人度过了许多忧郁凝重的时光，这是我永生难以忘怀的。但是，我却说不清楚他缠着我、领着我读的是些什么书，做的是些什么事。一种极度亢奋、完全失常的胡思乱想，使一切都蒙上了一层硫黄的微光，他即兴奏出的大段大段的挽歌，将永远在我耳畔回响。其中，我格外痛楚地记得，他对冯·韦伯的那首狂放的《最后的华尔兹》做了奇特的变异和夸张。他凭借他精巧的想象构思的一幅幅画面，在他的笔触下变得模糊不清，令我不寒而栗，而我因为不知道自己为何颤抖，就更感到格外恐怖。这些绘画（如今历历在目，依然鲜明），尽管我费尽心机，也只能表达出原本就属于书面语言范畴的那一小部分。他用极为简单的构图，用完全袒露的笔触，吸引和震慑着别人的注意力。如果世上曾经有人把思想绘诸笔端，那个人一定是罗德里克·厄歇尔。至少对于处在当时那种环境中的我来说，看到这位抑郁症患者企图在画布上表现的纯粹抽象的东西，我就感到一种难以忍受的强烈的恐惧，以前我在端详富塞利那些色彩十分艳丽但造型过于具体的幻想构图时，也未曾有过这种恐惧的感觉。

在我这位朋友的那些幻影幢幢的构图中，有一个倒

是不那么绝对抽象，可以勉强用文字描述一个大概。这是一幅小画，描绘了一个其长无比的矩形地窖或隧道的内部，内壁低矮，光滑，呈白色，没有间断，也没有装饰。从画面上的某些陪衬物可以看出，这个洞穴处于地底深处。长长的地道无限延伸，四周不见一个出口，也没有火炬和其他人造光源；但是却有一道耀眼的强光滚过整个空间，使一切沐浴在诡谲可怖、突兀怪异的光辉之中。

我在上文已经提到他病态的听觉神经，一切音乐都令他无法忍受，只有用弦乐器奏出的某些曲调例外。也许，正是因为他只能局限于摆弄吉他，所以才弹得那么如梦似幻，空灵怪诞。但是他那些即兴曲的狂热流畅，却不能归结于这个原因。他的狂想曲的那些音符，那些歌词（他经常一边弹琴，一边即兴唱出押韵的歌词），都肯定是，也确实是他情绪镇静、精神集中时的产物，而我前面已经委婉地提到，这种现象只有在他拼命强颜欢笑时才会出现。我很容易就记住了其中一首狂想曲的歌词。也许，他当初弹唱这支曲子时给我的印象最为强烈，因为我幻想自己从那潜在、隐秘的含义中第一次觉察出，厄歇尔已经充分意识到他那高高在上的理智正摇摇欲坠。

这首《闹鬼的宫殿》的歌词大致如下，也许记录得并非完全准确：

一

幽幽溪谷一片绿色葱茏，
曾有仁慈天使聚居其中，
还有一座宫殿气势恢宏——
金碧辉煌，傲然耸向苍穹。
在“思想”统治的国度里，
那座宫殿挺拔屹立！
就连展翅高飞的仙女，
也从未领略如此的美丽。

二

黄色的旗幡金光夺目，
在宫殿屋顶迎风飘舞，
（这一切的一切皆成虚无，
归于一去不返的远古）
在往昔甜蜜的岁月里，
阵阵微风在欢闹嬉戏，

沿着宫殿那粉白的墙壁，
有一缕幽香悠然飘去。

三

游子来到美丽的溪谷，
透过两扇明亮的窗户，
看见精灵们翩翩起舞，
和着琵琶柔美的旋律；
中间有个帝王气宇轩昂，
威严端坐在宝座之上！
他威风凛凛，通体辉煌，
俨然是一副国君之相。

四

珍珠美玉闪耀着光芒，
镶嵌在华丽的宫殿门上，
一群群回声你来我往，
在宫门间穿梭、飘荡，
回音女神的唯一职责，
就是唱出甜蜜的颂歌，

用曼妙绝伦的歌喉，

赞美帝王的足智多谋。

五

但是有恶魔身披黑衣，

闯入帝王高贵的领地；

（呜呼哀哉，帝王命毙！

让我们祝他永远安息）

昔日王宫的荣华富贵，

嫣红姹紫的夺目光辉，

如今随光阴一去无回，

宛若梦境萦绕在心扉。

六

如今游人来到这溪谷，

透过一扇扇猩红的窗户，

但见一些怪影狂野无主，

随着杂乱的旋律狂舞；

一群青面獠牙的鬼影，

像地狱之河湍急阴森，

穿过惨白无光的宫门，

不见笑容，只闻狂笑阵阵。

我清楚地记得，这首歌谣的意蕴曾引得我浮想联翩，厄歇尔的某个想法就在其中体现出来。我之所以提到这个想法，倒不是因为它新颖别致（其他人也有过类似的想法），而是因为厄歇尔始终对它执着不移。这种看法一般说来，就是认为花草树木皆有灵性。但是，在他狂乱的想象里，这种想法变得更加放纵，在某种特定的情况下竟拓展到了无机物的领域。我无法用语言来表达他对这一信条是何等执着，何等痴迷。但正如我前文所暗示的，他的信念与他祖先留下的这幢灰石房子有关。他想象着，那种灵性就具体表现在那些石头的排列顺序以及它们的安排规律上，在覆盖其上的大量苔藓上，在四周枯立的古树上，尤其表现在那种布局的永恒不变、始终如一之中，表现在那一湖死水的倒影之中。他说，在湖水和石墙周围逐渐凝聚着一团雾气，这便是证明——是那种灵性的证明，我听到这里，感到大为吃惊。他又补充说道，从那种寂然无声却又挥之不去的可怕的感染力上，可以见到那种灵性造成的后果，多少个世纪以来，

这感染力主宰着他们家族的命运，并使他变成眼前这副模样——我所看到的这副模样。对这类看法无须评论，我也不想妄做评论。

正如人们所能猜到的，我们读的书与这种幻想十分吻合，许多年来，这些书对病人的精神状态起了不小的作用。我们一同聚精会神地研读格雷塞的《翠鸟》和《修道院》，马基雅弗利的《魔鬼》，斯韦登堡的《天堂和地狱》，霍尔堡的《尼古拉·克里姆地下旅行记》，罗伯特·弗拉德、让·汤达日涅和德·拉·尚布尔各自所著的《手相术》，蒂克的《蓝色的旅程》，康帕内拉的《太阳城》。我们最喜欢的一本书是多明我会[1]教士艾梅里克·德·吉罗尼所著的八开本《宗教法庭手册》；而读了庞波尼乌斯·梅拉的有关古代非洲森林神和牧羊神的一些章节，厄歇尔经常会如痴如梦地呆坐几小时。不过，他最感兴趣的是一本极其珍贵的四开本哥特体孤本奇书——一座被湮没教堂的祈祷手册——《在马因斯教会礼堂追思亡灵》。

那天晚上，当厄歇尔突然告诉我玛德琳小姐已然过世，并说他打算把尸体先在府邸的一个地窖中存放十四

---

1. 多明我会，又名布道兄弟会，为天主教四大托钵修会之一，1215 年由西班牙托钵修士圣多明我（约 1170—1221）创立。——译者注

天之后再安葬时，我便不由自主地想起这本奇书中的荒唐仪式，以及它可能对这位忧郁症患者造成的影响。但是，他采取这一奇特做法也有其世俗的原因，我觉得不便贸然提出反对。他告诉我，他之所以这么决定，是考虑死者的病情不同一般，考虑到她那些医生会提出某些唐突的、刨根究底的疑问，还考虑到家族墓地偏僻荒凉，无人照看。当时我回想起我刚到厄歇尔府邸的那天，我在楼梯上遇见的那个人脸上的一副阴险表情，所以就无意反对他的做法，我认为这至少是一个没有害处、绝不算违背情理的防备措施。

应厄歇尔的请求，我亲自帮助他安排临时的入殓工作。尸体已经装入棺材，我们俩单独把它抬到停放处。停放尸体的那个地窖已经多年没有打开，我们的火把差点被令人窒息的空气熄灭，这使我们无法把里面查看清楚。只记得那个地窖窄小、潮湿，没有一点缝隙，透不进一丝光线，深深地埋在地下，上面正是我睡觉的那个房间。看来，在遥远的封建时代，那地窖曾被当作牢房，后来又作为贮存火药及其他易燃物品的地方，因为一部分地板和我们经过的整个长长的过道都仔细包裹着黄铜。那扇厚重的铁门也曾受到同样的保护。铁门因为沉重，

在铰链上旋转时发出异常刺耳的吱嘎声。

在那可怕的地窖里，我们把令人悲伤的棺材放在架子上，稍稍掀开尚未钉上的棺盖，瞻仰死者的遗容。我第一次注意到他们兄妹二人长得极为相似。厄歇尔大概看出了我的心思，喃喃地解释了几句，我这才知道他和死者是孪生兄妹，彼此之间有着一种简直难以理解的心灵感应。然而，我们的目光却不敢在死者身上久留，因为看了不免心生恐惧。疾病就这样夺去了这位妙龄女子的生命，她像所有强直性晕厥症患者一样，胸口和脸上泛着一抹似真似假的红晕，一缕令人生疑的微笑在她唇角逗留不去，看上去十分可怕。我们把棺盖重新盖好，钉上钉子，然后关好铁门，迈着沉重的步伐，回到几乎和地窖同样阴暗凄凉的地面。

在度过几个悲痛欲绝的日子之后，我的朋友精神错乱的一些特征出现了显著的变化。平常的那副举止消失不见了。平常所做的事情也被他搁置一边或忘到脑后。他迈着慌慌张张、踉踉跄跄的步子，漫无目的地从一个房间徘徊到另一个房间。苍白的脸色变得更加惨白吓人，而眼里的光芒却熄灭无踪了。以往那种不时沙哑的嗓音不再听到；现在他的声音习惯性地颤抖不停，仿佛内心

充满极度的恐惧。确实，有的时候，我认为他那终日惶恐不安的心里藏着某个令他窒息的秘密，他正在拼命积蓄足够的勇气，把它吐露出来。而有的时候，我又不得不把这一切当成莫名其妙的疯狂的胡思乱想，因为我看见他一连几小时两眼聚精会神地凝视空茫，仿佛在倾听冥冥之中的某个声音。也无怪他的这副状况令我害怕，令我也受到感染。我觉得他那种荒诞癫狂、动人心魄的迷信，正在缓慢而明确地潜入我的心头。

尤其是在我们把玛德琳小姐放置在地窖七八天后的一个深夜，我躺在床上更为真切地体会到这种情绪的影响。我辗转反侧不能入睡，而时间却在一小时一小时地流逝。我拼命排解，想驱散盘踞在我心头的紧张不安。我强迫自己相信，我的紧张多半（如果不是全部）是由于房间里沉闷的家具对我产生了令人惶惑的影响——由于那暗淡破旧的帷幔，随着即将来临的风暴的吹动，在墙上来回摆动，摩擦着床上的装饰布，发出骚乱不安的窸窸窣窣的声音。但是我的排解无济于事。一阵难以抑制的战栗渐渐传遍我的全身，最后，一种噩梦一般的无名的恐惧占据了我的心房。我喘着气，挣扎着摆脱出来，从枕头上抬起身子，仔细凝视漆黑一片的房间，屏息倾

听——我不知道为何倾听，除非是受到本能驱使——倾听某种低微而模糊的声音，它在风暴暂停的间歇响起，却不知道从何处传来。我被一种不可名状、难以忍受的极度的恐惧所震慑，慌忙穿上衣服（我感到那天夜里我不能再睡了），开始在房间里匆匆地踱来踱去，努力想使自己摆脱那凄楚可怜的境地。

我就这样来回踱了几圈，突然附近楼梯上传来一阵轻微的脚步声，引起了我的注意。我很快听出这是厄歇尔的脚步声。紧接着，他轻轻敲了敲我的房门，端着一盏灯走了进来。他的脸色和平时一样惨白，但眼睛里却闪耀着一种疯狂的喜悦——一举一动都带着显然经过压抑的歇斯底里。他的这副神情令我毛骨悚然——但是，比起我独守长夜那份孤独来，什么都是好的，我甚至把他的光临看作缓解我孤独的救星。

“怎么，你还没有看见？”他一声不吭地四下盯视片刻，突然说道，“你还没有看见？——啊，等一等，你会看见的。”他一边说着，一边仔细把灯遮上，然后匆匆走到一扇窗户跟前，猛地将它推开，迎向外面的风暴。

一阵猛烈的强风刮进来，差点吹得我们站不稳脚跟。这一夜虽然狂风呼啸，却是异常美丽，是一个奇特

的、交织着恐惧和美丽的夜晚。一股旋风显然已在附近聚集起力量，因为风向不时发生剧烈变化；沉重的乌云低低垂悬，仿佛压向府邸的塔楼；乌云尽管浓重，我们仍能看见云块从四面八方涌来，带着充沛的活力挤压碰撞，却并不飘向远方。我是说乌云尽管浓重，我们仍能看见这幅景象，但却不见月亮和星星，也不见闪电的影子。但是在大团大团翻滚涌动的云雾下面，在我们附近地面上的一切物体上面，闪耀着一种微弱而又清晰的雾气散发出的奇异的白光，这雾气笼罩着宅屋，像裹尸布一样把它覆盖。

“你不能看！你绝不能看！”我战战兢兢地对厄歇尔说，一边轻轻用力把他从窗口拖到一张椅子上。“这些使你迷惑的景象不过是普通的电光现象，也许是由于那小湖中瘴气弥漫所形成的。我们关上窗户吧。空气寒冷，对你的身体没有好处。这里有一本你最喜欢的传奇小说，我来念，你听着，我们就这样共同度过这个恐怖的夜晚吧。”

我随手拿起的那本旧书是劳斯洛特·坎宁先生所著的《疯狂的宴会》，我称它为厄歇尔最爱读的书，不过是无奈中的一句言不由衷的调侃。因为说实话，这本书语

言粗俗，想象贫乏，故事拖沓，我这位品味高雅、精神世界丰富的朋友是不会对它感兴趣的。然而，当时手头只有这么一本书，我怀有一种侥幸心理，希望那些搅得这位忧郁症患者惶恐不安的激动情绪，能在我所读的荒唐透顶的故事中得到缓解（精神错乱的病史上有许多类似的奇特病例）。确实，如果我当时能从他听故事（或表面上在听）时那副紧张压抑的狂喜上做出判断，我就真可以庆幸自己妙计得逞了。

我已经读到人们所熟悉的那一段情节，宴会的主人埃瑟尔雷德千方百计想和平进入隐士的居所，却始终没有成功，便开始靠武力强行闯入。记得书里是这样叙述这段情节的：

> 埃瑟尔雷德性情本就刚烈勇猛。加之畅饮后酒性发作，就更加气势逼人，他不再同那顽固不化的歹毒隐士多费口舌。这时他感到雨点落在他的肩头，担心暴风雨就要来临，立时抡起钉头槌，狠狠砸了几下，转眼将门板凿了个窟窿，再把套着臂铠的胳膊伸进去，使劲一拉，那扇门顿时四分五裂，木板折断破裂时发出干

燥空洞令人心惊胆寒的声音，在森林里久久回荡。

念完这最后一句，我猛吃一惊，停住了。我仿佛听到（尽管立刻断定是我情绪激动产生的幻觉）——我仿佛隐隐约约地听到——从府邸中某个偏僻的角落传来一个声音，听上去和劳斯洛特先生格外详细描写的那破门的回声极为相似，只是更加沉闷、模糊。毫无疑问，正是这种巧合吸引了我的注意。在窗框啪嗒啪嗒的撞击声和外面一阵紧似一阵的狂风呼啸声中，这声音实在不算什么，不会使我感兴趣，也不会使我惶恐不安。我继续把故事念下去：

好汉埃瑟尔雷德破门而入后，却不见那个歹毒隐士的踪影，这使他既恼怒又惊讶。却只见一条满身鳞片、口吐火舌的巨龙，镇守着一座黄金建造、白银铺地的宫殿，墙上挂着一副闪闪发光的铜盾，上面镌刻着两行铭文：

进宝殿者成霸主；

屠巨龙者赢盾牌。

> 埃瑟尔雷德高高抡起钉头槌，一下击中龙头。龙头滚落在他脚下，喷出一口毒气，发出一声令人发指的尖厉刺耳的惨叫，埃瑟尔雷德只好用双手捂住耳朵，这声音实在是撕心裂肺，前所未闻。

念到这里，我又猝然停住，心中大为愕然——这次再也无法怀疑了。我确确实实听见（尽管我发现我很难说出这声音来自何方）一个微弱、遥远，但却尖厉刺耳的惨叫声或摩擦声，悠长不绝，诡谲离奇——我读着书中的描写，心里已然想象出巨龙的那声石破天惊的惨叫，而耳边听到的这个声音，正跟我的想象不差分毫。

这个无比怪异的声音，这种最最离奇的巧合，自然使我心头产生无数种互相矛盾的感觉，直压得我喘不过气来，其中最令我不堪忍受的是极度的惊愕和恐惧，但我仍然保持着足够的镇静，以免出言不慎，刺激了我这位朋友敏感的神经。我不敢肯定他是否听见这些声音，不过在刚刚几分钟内，他的举止确实发生了奇怪的变化。他原来坐在我对面，现在却已将椅子慢慢挪开，面对房门坐着。这样一来，我只能看到他脸的局部，只见他双

唇颤抖不已，仿佛在无声地喃喃自语。他的脑袋耷拉在胸口，但我知道他并没有睡着，从侧面也能看到他两眼大睁，一眨不眨。他身体的动作也证明他没有睡着，他一直在不停地轻轻左右摇晃。我把这一切看在眼里，继续念劳斯洛特先生的故事，情节如下：

> 却说那好汉摆脱了巨龙的魔爪，猛然想到墙上的铜盾，想到要打破上面所附的魔咒，于是他搬开挡在前面的巨龙尸体，英勇无畏地踏过城堡的白银地面，走向挂着铜盾的那面墙壁。可实际上，没等他来到墙边，铜盾就掉落在他脚边的白银地面上，发出一声可怕的巨响，震耳欲聋。

我刚刚念出这几个字，仿佛在那一刹那，真的有一面铜盾重重摔落在白银地面上一样——我听到一阵金属撞击的声音，清晰，空洞，却又显得沉闷压抑。我大惊失色，一跃而起；厄歇尔却依旧坐在椅子里晃来晃去。我冲到他的椅子跟前，只见他双眼怔怔地凝视前方，整个表情像石头一般僵硬。但是，当我把手放在他的肩头

时，他浑身一阵剧烈的震颤，嘴唇哆嗦着露出一个惨笑。我看见他颤抖着喃喃自语，声音又低又急，仿佛不知道我就在跟前。我弯腰向他靠近，终于听见了他话里的可怕含义。

“现在听见了吧？——是的，我听见了，我早就听见了。好久——好久——好久——好几分钟，好几小时，好几天以前，我就听见了——可是我不敢——哦，可怜可怜我吧，我是多么可怜啊！——我不敢——我不敢说啊！我们把她活埋啦！我不是说过我感觉敏锐吗？现在我告诉你，她在空洞洞的棺材里最初发出的微弱响动我都听见了。我听见了——好多好多天以前——可是我不敢——我不敢说啊！现在——今天夜里——埃瑟尔雷德——哈！哈哈！——撞破隐士的房门，巨龙临死的惨叫，盾牌落地的巨响——唉，那还不如说是她棺材的劈裂声，她牢房里铁铰链的摩擦声，和她在包着黄铜的地窖走廊里拼命挣扎的声音！啊！我逃到哪里去呢？她不是很快就会上这儿来吗？她不是正在匆匆赶来责备我行事仓促？我不是已经听见她的脚步踏上楼梯？我不是已经听出她的心脏在沉重而可怕地跳动？疯子！”说到这里，他疯狂地一跃而起，仿佛拼足了全身的气力，尖声

怪叫着说:“疯子！我告诉你，她此刻就站在门外！”

似乎他那蕴含超凡力量的叫喊中真的有一股魔力，只见他用手指着那道宽大古老的房门，在刹那间，那两扇沉重的乌木门扉竟然徐徐打开了。这一定是狂风将它吹开的。但是，就在那两扇门外，果真站着厄歇尔家玛德琳小姐那体形高大、裹着尸衣的身影。她那白色的尸衣上血迹斑斑，瘦骨嶙峋的身体的每一部分都有苦苦挣扎过的痕迹。她浑身颤抖着，摇摇晃晃地站在门槛上，然后，随着一声低幽的呜咽，重重地跌进屋来，倒在她哥哥身上，一阵剧烈的、临终前的挣扎，把他也拖拽到地上，成为一具死尸，成为他曾经预料过的恐怖的牺牲品。

我吓得魂飞魄散，逃离了那个房间，逃离了那座宅屋。当我穿过那古老的堤道时，风暴仍然在疯狂肆虐。突然，沿着堤道射来一道耀眼的光芒，我转过身来，想看看这种不同寻常的光芒从何而来，因为我的身后只有那高大的府邸和它的影子。原来光芒来自那一轮正在西沉的血红色的满月，月光鲜明地照亮了我前文中提到的那道原来不易察觉的，从屋顶弯弯曲曲延伸至墙脚的裂缝。就在我凝视的时候，这道裂缝迅速变宽，随着一阵

旋风呼啸着吹过，那轮圆满的红月亮赫然呈现在我眼前，我头晕目眩地看到宅屋那高大的墙壁纷纷坍塌，耳边传来一阵骚乱的喊叫。经久不息，仿佛十万个浪头在翻滚咆哮，而我脚下那黑暗幽深的小湖，沉闷地、寂无声息地淹没了已成碎石瓦砾的“厄歇尔府”。

一桶白葡萄酒

福图纳托对我一而再再而三的伤害，我都能忍就忍了，可是他竟然敢侮辱我，我便发誓要报仇雪恨了。你这么了解我的脾气禀性，肯定知道我不会公开发出威胁。我最后必定要报仇雪恨，这是板上钉钉的事——但是报仇绝不能带来任何风险，这也是确凿无疑的。我不仅要惩罚对方，还要让自己不受惩罚。如果修正错误的人受到惩罚，那错误就得不到修正。如果复仇者没有让自己感觉到已经惩罚了做坏事的人，那错误也得不到修正。

你必须明白，我在语言和行为上，都没有给福图纳托任何理由来怀疑我的善良愿望。我继续按我的老习惯冲他微笑，他没有看出，我现在的笑容里藏着置他于死

地的想法。

这位福图纳托老兄有一个弱点——在其他方面他倒是个令人尊敬甚至让人害怕的男人。他很为自己在葡萄酒方面的鉴赏力感到得意。意大利人很少具有真正的大师气质。在大多数情况下，他们的热情都只是逢场作戏，骗骗那些英国和美国的百万富翁。在绘画和宝石的领域，福图纳托跟他的同胞一样，是个江湖骗子，但是在陈年佳酿的问题上，他的态度十分认真。我在这方面跟他没有本质的区别——我本人对意大利葡萄酒也很精通，只要有可能就大量地购买。

话说，这是嘉年华到达癫狂顶峰的一个傍晚，我和我的朋友不期而遇。他过分热情地跟我搭话，因为他当时已经喝了不少。这家伙身上的衣服像个大杂烩。紧身的条纹衫，头上是一顶圆锥形的帽子，上面还挂着许多小铃铛。我见到他太高兴了，紧攥着他的手怎么也不肯松开。

我对他说:“亲爱的福图纳托，碰到你真是太巧了。你今天看上去气色很不错。我得到了一大桶好货，据说是阿蒙蒂亚多白葡萄酒，但我对此心存疑虑。”

“怎么会？”他说，“阿蒙蒂亚多？一大桶？不可

能！而且是在嘉年华期间！”

“我心存疑虑，”我回答道，“当时我头脑发昏，没有征求一下你对此的看法，就按阿蒙蒂亚多的价钱付了全款。我那时候找不到你，又担心丢了一笔好买卖。”

“阿蒙蒂亚多！”

“我心存疑虑。”

“阿蒙蒂亚多！”

“我必须让他们满意。”

“阿蒙蒂亚多！”

“既然你有事在身，我这会儿正要去找卢切里西，有评论家天赋的人非他莫属。他会告诉我——”

“卢切里西根本分不清阿蒙蒂亚多酒和雪利酒。”

“可是有些傻瓜竟然说他的品位跟你不相上下。”

“快，我们走吧。”

“去哪儿？”

“去你的地下室。”

“不行，我的朋友。我不能因为你脾气好就强人所难。我看出你有应酬。卢切里西——”

“我没有应酬——快走吧。”

“我的朋友，不行啊。不是因为应酬，是我发现你

正遭受重感冒的折磨。而地下室里潮湿得令人无法忍受。墙壁上都结了硝石。”

“我们还是走吧。感冒没什么大不了的。阿蒙蒂亚多！你准是受骗上当了。至于卢切里西，他根本就分不清雪利酒和阿蒙蒂亚多。”

这么说着话，福图纳托一把抓住了我的胳膊。我戴上一个黑色丝绸面罩，用一件短披风把身体紧紧裹住，他一个劲儿地催着我去我的豪华寝宫。

家里没有侍者，他们都逃出去过节，去寻欢作乐了。我跟他们说过我要次日早晨才回来，我还明确地命令他们不许离开家门。我心里很清楚，这些命令能有效地保证他们全都在我刚一转身就消失得无影无踪。

我从他们的烛台上拿了两根蜡烛，递了一根给福图纳托，前倨后恭地领他穿过几个套间，走向通往地下室的那道拱门。我走下一条长长的旋转楼梯，请求他跟上时多加小心。最后，我们来到了楼梯底部，一起站在蒙特雷索尔地下墓穴的潮湿的地面上。

我朋友的步子踉踉跄跄，帽子上的铃铛随着他的脚步叮叮作响。

“那桶酒。”他说。

“还得再往前走一点，”我说，“可是，你仔细看看这些洞穴墙壁上的亮晶晶的网状物。”

他转向我，盯着我的眼睛，他两个浑浊的眼球上渗出了迷醉的泪水。

“硝石？”他终于问道。

“硝石。”我回答道，“你那样咳嗽多久了？”

“喀！喀！喀！……喀！喀！喀！……喀！喀！喀！……喀！喀！喀！……喀！喀！喀！”

我可怜的朋友发现他好几分钟没法儿回答我的话。

“没关系。”他最后说道。

“走，”我果断地说，“我们回去吧，你的健康最宝贵。你富有，受人尊敬，受人景仰，受人爱戴。你是幸福的，就像我曾经一样。你是一个不可或缺的人。至于我嘛，根本不值一提。我们回去吧。你会生病的，这个责任我可负不起。而且，还有卢切里西——”

“够了，”他说，“咳嗽根本不算什么，要不了我的命。我不会因为咳嗽而丢了性命。”

“不错——不错，”我回答道，“其实，我也并没打算毫无必要地让你感到紧张——但是你应该保持适当的谨慎。喝一口这种梅多克红葡萄酒吧，它能帮助我们抵抗

潮湿。”

说到这里，我从放在地面上的一长排酒瓶里抽出一瓶，敲掉了它的瓶颈。

“喝吧。”我说着，把葡萄酒递给他。

他乜斜着眼睛，把酒端到唇边。他顿了顿，冲我亲切地点了点头，那些铃铛发出叮叮的声音。

“我敬这些在我们周围安息的死者。”他说。

“我祝你长命百岁。”

他又一次抓住我的胳膊，我们继续往前走。

“这些地下室，”他说，“规模很大。”

“蒙特雷索尔，”我说，“是一个庞大的、人丁兴旺的家族。”

“我忘记你们的纹章是什么了。”

“一只巨大的金色人脚，底色是天蓝色。人脚踏碎了一条凶猛的蛇，蛇牙扎进了脚后跟。”

“铭词是什么？”

“凡伤我者必受惩罚。”[1]

“很好！”他说。

葡萄酒在他眼睛里闪烁，那些铃铛叮叮作响。我自

1. 原文为拉丁语。——译者注

己的想象也因梅多克红葡萄酒而有了温度。我们经过长长的墙壁，墙边堆着骷髅，大大小小的酒桶混杂其间，然后我们进入地下墓穴的最深的凹处。我又停了下来，这次冒昧地抓住了福图纳托一只胳膊的肘部上面。

“硝石！”我说，“看见了吗？越来越多了。像青苔一样挂在拱顶上。我们是在河床的下面了。湿气凝成的水珠在骨头间流淌。快，趁现在还来得及，我们回去吧。你的咳嗽——”

“那不算什么，”他说，“我们继续往前走吧。但是先给我再来一杯梅多克葡萄酒。”

我停住话头，给他拿了一瓶“坟墓诱惑”。他一饮而尽。他的眼睛里闪着灼热的光。他哈哈大笑，把酒瓶往上一扔，那姿势我看着有点奇怪。

我惊讶地看着他。他又做了一遍那个动作——十分怪异。

“你不懂吗？”他说。

“不懂。”我回答。

“看来你不是兄弟会的。”

“这怎么讲？”

“你不是瓦匠会的。”

“我是，我是，”我说，“我是瓦匠会的。”

“你？不可能！你是瓦匠？”

“我是瓦匠。”我回答。

“给个证明，”他说，“给个证明。”

“这就是。”我回答，从短风衣的褶皱中掏出一把泥刀。

“你开玩笑。”他惊叫道，向后退了几步，“不过，还是让我们继续去找阿蒙蒂亚多吧。”

“好的。”我说，把泥刀塞回短风衣下面，又让他挽住我的胳膊。他把沉重的身体靠在我胳膊上，我们继续前进，去寻找阿蒙蒂亚多。我们经过一连串低矮的拱门，往下，继续往前，再往下，来到一个很深的地下墓穴，里面浑浊的空气使我们的两根蜡烛不再燃烧，只发出一点微弱的亮光。

在地下墓穴的最远端，出现了另一个面积较小的墓穴。四壁堆着人类的遗骨，依照巴黎的地下墓穴的式样，一直堆到上面的拱顶。这个内部墓穴，三面墙都按这种风格装饰。第四面墙的遗骨坍塌了下来，乱七八糟地倒在地上，在某一处形成了相当大的一堆。因为遗骨的坍塌，我们看见墙里面是另一个内部墓穴或密室，深约四

英尺，宽三英尺，高六七英尺。它似乎本身没有什么特殊的用途，只是在两根巨大的柱子之间形成了间隔，这两根柱子和其他柱子一起支撑起整个地下墓穴的顶部，密室的后部是坚实的花岗岩围墙。

福图纳托举起手里黯淡的蜡烛，努力想窥探这间密室的深处，可是没有成功。烛光太微弱了，我们无法看清密室的尽头。

“继续往前，”我说，“阿蒙蒂亚多就在这里面。那个卢切里西——”

“他是个无知的人。”我的朋友打断了我的话，继续踉踉跄跄地往前走，我立刻紧紧地跟上。一眨眼，他就来到了密室的尽头，发现被岩石挡住，没法儿再往前走了，他就一脸迷惑，呆呆地站在那儿。片刻之后，我就把他拴在了花岗岩上。花岗岩的表面有两个 U 形铁钉，在同一高度，相距大约两英尺。一个铁钉上挂着一根短短的链条，另一根铁钉上有个挂锁。我把链条从他的腰部甩过去，只用了几秒钟就把锁牢牢地锁住了。他完全被惊呆了，根本无力抵抗。我拔出钥匙，从密室里退了出来。

“把你的手，”我说，“放在墙上，你会忍不住摸那

些硝石。这里确实非常潮湿。我再一次恳求你回去。不回？那么我必须果断地离开你了。但是我首先必须尽我所能对你表示一些关注。”

“阿蒙蒂亚多！”我的朋友突然喊道，还没有从他的惊愕中醒过神来。

“没错，”我回答道，“阿蒙蒂亚多。”

我一边说这句话，一边让我自己置身于前面说过的那堆尸骨中间。我把尸骨拨拉到旁边，很快就发现了大量的建筑石料和砂浆。我在那把泥刀的帮助下，开始充满干劲地用这些材料堵塞密室的入口。

我刚砌好第一层石料，就发现福图纳托的醉意大大地消退了。关于这点，我得到的最初迹象是密室深处传来一声低低的、呻吟般的喊叫。这不是一个醉汉的喊叫。在这之后是很长时间的顽强的沉默。我砌上第二层石料，然后是第三层、第四层，然后我听见链条在剧烈地摇晃。这声音持续了几分钟，在这期间，我停下手头的活儿，坐在那些尸骨上，让自己听得更加心满意足。最后，金属的碰撞声平静下来，我重新拿起泥刀，一口气砌完了第五层、第六层和第七层石料。现在石墙差不多到我胸口了。我又停下来，把蜡烛举到石墙上方，让几道微弱

的亮光投向里面的那个身影。

一连串响亮而凄厉的尖叫，突然从那个被链条拴住的人影的嗓子里发出，像一记重拳把我打了回来。在那短短的一瞬间，我迟疑了，我颤抖了。我拔出我的长剑，开始用它在密室里探索，可是突然一个闪念，使我放下心来。我把手放在地下墓穴坚实的墙体上，心里感到很踏实。我再一次走近石墙，对那个拼命吵闹的人的叫嚷做出回答。我重复他的喊叫，给他推波助澜，在音量和力度上都超越他的喊声。我这么做了之后，里面的喊叫声就平静了下来。

时间已是午夜，我的任务快要完成了。我已经砌完了第八层、第九层和第十层石料。第十一层是最后一层，我也砌好了一部分，现在只要把最后一块石头填进去，再抹上砂浆，就大功告成了。我挣扎着搬起沉重的石料，把它的一部分塞进那个注定的位置。然而，此时从密室里传来一声低笑，吓得我头发都竖了起来。低笑之后，一个悲哀的声音说话了，我好不容易才辨认出那是高贵的福图纳托的声音。只听那声音说道：

“哈！哈！哈！嘿！嘿！嘿！真是一个很有意思的恶作剧——一个精彩的玩笑。我们可以在寝宫里喝着葡萄

酒——嘿！嘿！嘿！——拿这件事情笑个够了——嘿！嘿！嘿！”

“阿蒙蒂亚多！”我说。

“嘿！嘿！嘿！……嘿！嘿！嘿！……没错，阿蒙蒂亚多。不过时间是不是很晚了？他们，福图纳托夫人和其他人，会不会在宫殿里等我们？我们离开吧。”

“好的，”我说，“我们离开吧。”

“为了上帝的爱，蒙特雷索尔！”

“是的，”我说，“为了上帝的爱！”

可是我没有听到对我这句话的回答。我失去了耐心，大声喊道：“福图纳托！”

没有回答。我再次喊道：“福图纳托！”

还是没有回答。我把一根蜡烛伸进最后那个缺口，让它落了下去。里面只传来一阵叮叮的铃铛声。我感到心里难受，这都是地下墓穴的潮湿造成的。我匆匆把手头的活儿干完。我把最后一块石料用力塞进去，用砂浆把它抹平。我把那些古老的尸骨重新垒在新砌的石墙边。半个世纪以来，没有一个活人过来打扰过它们。愿死者的灵魂安息！

企鹅经典：小黑书　第一辑

01. 贝尔科洛蕾夫人与神父
[意] 薄伽丘

02. 泄密的心
[美] 爱伦 · 坡

03. 醋栗
[俄] 契诃夫

04. 一个人需要许多土地吗？
[俄] 列夫 · 托尔斯泰

05. 一颗简单的心
[法] 福楼拜

06. 傻子的一生
[日] 芥川龙之介

07. 萎缩的胳膊
[英] 托马斯 · 哈代

08. 樱花树下的清酒
[日] 吉田兼好

09. 虎！虎！
[英] 威廉 · 布莱克

10. 给一个青年诗人的十封信
[奥] 里尔克

Penguin Little Black Classics Vol. I

01. GIOVANNI BOCCACCIO
Mrs Rosie and the Priest

02. EDGAR ALLAN POE
The Tell-Tale Heart

03. ANTON CHEKHOV
Gooseberries

04. LEO TOLSTOY
How Much Land Does a Man Need?

05. GUSTAVE FLAUBERT
A Simple Heart

06. RYUNOSUKE AKUTAGAWA
The Life of a Stupid Man

07. THOMAS HARDY
The Withered Arm

08. KENKO
A Cup of Sake Beneath the Cherry Trees

09. WILLIAM BLAKE
Tyger Tyger

10. RAINER MARIA RILKE
Letters to a Young Poet

PENGUIN

LITTLE BLACK

CLASSICS